GOOD OLD ERNIE

Marian R. Bartch
and
Jerry J. Mallett

A Perma-Bound Book

Hertzberg—New Method, Inc.   *Jacksonville, Illinois*

A Hardcover Edition of *Good Old Ernie* is published
by Carlton Press.
Published by arrangement with the authors.
First PERMA-BOUND Edition: September, 1983.

GOOD
OLD
ERNIE

CHAPTER ONE

I, Ernestine Cecelia Tubb (Ernie to my friends, Tubby to my enemies), have lived in little Pleasant Valley for a long, long time. Well, maybe you wouldn't consider eleven years a long time, but then you probably haven't been living the same kind of life I have ... at least, I hope not! It's the rotten things that keep happening to me that make those eleven years seem like more than an ordinary kid's lifetime. Unusual things do happen to me for no apparent reason, through no fault of my own, I'm sure. It's hard to understand.

So, here I am, living in little old Pleasant Valley .... all these years ... all these rotten experiences! Boy ... if ever a place was given the wrong name, it's Pleasant Valley. This place is far from pleasant. In fact, I have found it to be just the opposite ... unpleasant! If I had a penny, not a dollar, but a penny, mind you, for every dumb thing that has happened to me during my eleven years in this place, I would be the richest girl in the whole U. S. of A.

My family and all of my friends think of me as a nice, easy-going, even-tempered, cheerful kind of person, able to handle whatever comes my way with no fusss ... "good, old Ernie, solid as the rock of Gibraltar!" whatever that means. Well, I guess that shows what a great little actress I really am. I ought to be starring in my own television series ... "Ernie, the Great!" or something. If those people only knew how many times I could have just curled up and died of embarrassment and shame, or would have been only too glad to sink into the quicksand on Louise's farm ...

5

It's my family, you see. We are not exactly what is considered to be a normal, conventional, all-American family group. We might be in your town, I don't know, but we certainly are not considered so here in Pleasant Valley. And it's not just the problem of trying to cope with my ding-bat of a little sister, Bitsey, either. A kid sort of expects a brother or sister to be creepy, repulsive, even a real nuisance, and Bitsey has never disappointed me in that respect. For example, let me tell you how she got her name. Her real name is Barbara Ann Tubb, but everybody has called her "Bitsey" since the day she bit the minister in the leg as he was standing in the vestibule of the church greeting the members of the congregation after the service. Dad laughed at her "cuteness" all the way home, and, in spite of Mom's disapproval, the name stuck. Personally, I think that Fido or Rover would have suited her better and said so when I asked my parents if the minister would have to have a rabies shot, but my comments weren't a bit appreciated by either of them. Bitsey may be only three years old, but she's a terror . . . has to be watched all the time!

Well, a kid can take that kind of a sister if she has the right kind of parents. . .serious, considerate of their older daughter. . .conventional. But does Ernestine Cecelia Tubb have that kind of parents? Are you kidding? I just happen to have what may be, what most certainly is, the most mixed-up set of parents a kid ever got stuck with. . .and I mean stuck! I must have been born under the wrong sign of the Zodiac or something. I know I was born into the wrong family. Either that or my parents picked up the wrong baby at the hospital! I often wonder about that.

But nothing, nothing that has ever happened to me can begin to compare with what happened to our family, especially to me, this past year. You will not, will not believe what my parents did for one whole, absolute, entire, complete, cotton-picking year. No, they didn't abandon us to go on a world cruise—better if they had! What they did was—are you ready—what they did was to trade jobs. Yes, that's right. . .trade jobs! Dad became "Mom" staying home to manage the house and look after the family's needs, while Mom became "Dad" and went to work running our family's hardware store every day. A simple thing, you say? A neat exchange? No, it was not a simple thing. No, it was not a neat exchange. No other family in the whole of Pleasant Valley would be foolish enough to live the way our family did this year. No other parents would subject their hard-working, deserving-of-a-better-life daughter (me, Ernestine) to all of the indignities I had to needlessly suffer because of their dumb job switch.

Let me tell you now about this wild, crazy, mixed-up year. It all began on a hot, humid, storm-threatening day in August. . .the perfect atmosphere for what was to come. . .

CHAPTER TWO

"Water. . . water. . .water . . ." I called in a thirst-weakened voice. Oh, I was so thirsty. . .oh, my throat's so parched. The heat was burning my eyes. I could barely see for the tears that were streaming down my feverish face. How did I ever get into this desert? What am I doing here? How will I ever get out? Oh. . .it's so hot. . .so hot. I'm so thirsty. Water. . .water. . .water, I must have water. How long can I go on without water? Not much longer, I'm afraid, not much longer. Oh, now what's happened? Oh, no, I've lost one of my slippers in the sand. It's so hard to walk in the sand. . .the heat is scorching my foot. Must hurry. . .try to hurry. . .can't move fast enough. . .need water. Do I see an oasis? Or is it only a mirage? Now, I can't see anything—the hot, smothering wind is blowing sand in my face. . .sand all over me. . .blowing harder. . .blowing harder. . .harder. . .I'm falling down. . .down. . .down. . .into the depths of a fiery furnace. . .down. . .down. . .

WHAMP!! CLUNK!! THUD!!

"Ohhh. . .my head!" I groaned. I sat up and looked around—to my disbelief, I was in my own bedroom—but not in bed. . .on the floor. There I was, in a big heap. My arms and legs were all tangled up with the pillow, wadded-up sheet, and almost half the mattress! My pajamas were so soaking wet that they clung to me as tightly as if they were glued on. I then noticed a slight rustling of the curtains as a hot, dry, dusty breeze blew in. The sky was overcast—I could hear distant rumblings of thunder and see faint flashes of lightning in the sky.

"Well, Ernestine," I asked myself, "just how long are you going to sit here on the floor like a soggy cookie?" In answer, I got up and squished down the hall to the bathroom. I still needed water and knew that I could drink at least a dozen glasses, but was surprised to find that it only took three and a half glasses to fill me up, even thought my thirst wasn't entirely quenched. I figured there was only one place in the world hotter than Pleasant Valley in August. . .Death Valley! One of the *most* unpleasant things about Pleasant Valley was the intense heat that closed in on you during the month of August—hot, humid, almost suffocating. About the only way

9

to get any relief, actually the only way to survive, is to spend your days floating in the Pleasant Valley Community Swimming Pool. I really have a burning hatred for that pool, and you'll soon understand why, but going there is the only way to keep comparatively cool.

I thought that maybe some orange juice would taste good, so I threw on a pair of shorts and a shirt and hurried down to the kitchen. On the way I tripped over Chief Bitsey's firetruck in the downstairs hall, so I had to hold my bruised toe in one hand and hop all the rest of the way. I knew Mom and Dad were already up because I could hear them arguing in the kitchen. I wondered what was up now. My parents have very few arguments, but when they do. . .oh, boy!

Dad was saying, "I didn't mean to insinuate that what you do around here isn't important. . .of course it is, in its way. It's just that you are able to have a nice, easy, relaxed day, working on your own time schedule. You don't have the pressures of a *full-time* job like I do—or the responsibilities. You simply have no idea of what it's like to try to get along with and please fussy, difficult customers every day all day long. To say nothing about the salesmen, and the late orders, and. . ."

"Oh, so you don't think running a house and looking after a practically helpless husband, and two little girls is a full-time job!" interrupted Mom. "You don't think I have any pressures, any difficult people to cope with, any schedules to keep up with. What do you think—that I live in a vacuum all day long? Well, anytime that you'd like to trade jobs, Buster, just you let me know! I'm the one who needs a good, restful vacation. I would really enjoy spending some time loafing around the store, gossiping with the customers, going for coffee with the salesmen, yes, I sure would like a change like that."

"Morning," I said.

"Loafing. . .gossiping. . .I can't believe what I'm hearing," replied Dad. "You've seen me coming home every evening, tired, exhausted after a long day of slaving at the store, working hard just trying to provide some luxuries for my little family. Like some of the new appliances I bought for you, to make your work easier—to keep you from being as tired and worn-out from working as I am."

10

"Morning, folks," I said again. I was beginning to feel like the invisible child.

"You sound like a soap opera," returned Mom. "Now I know where Ernie gets her sense of the dramatic."

Well, at least Mom remembered I did exist, even if she didn't seem able to see me at that moment. That was some comfort to me.

"I would just love to see you running that store for one week," was Dad's angry reply. "Just one week! Loafing! Gossiping!!"

"Run it for one week. . .ha!" retorted Mom in a loud voice (still ignoring me completely). "I could easily run it for one year and not have any problems. I'd love to see you trying to cope with the important problems that crop up around here. What about it? Are you afraid to try?"

I tried once more, "Good morning," raising my voice a little so I'd fit right in.

"Oh, come on, now," replied Dad, rising to the bait. "You surely don't believe that a grown man who has the practical experience and know-how for managing a complex business would have any problems in keeping a household organized, with doing simple little chores, do you?"

Nobody had paid any attention to my cheerful greeting

"I'd just like to see you try it," roared Mom. "Oh, oh," I thought, "Dad's done it now with his 'simple-little-chores' routine. It will take more than roses and a candlelight dinner to get out of this one."

"Oh, you would, would you?" shot back Dad.

I was seriously beginning to wonder if I was really there. The thought crossed my mind that I might still be dreaming. . .or maybe had gotten so hot sleeping in that blast furnace of a bedroom that I had melted away and was now only a ghostly voice, just faintly heard and never seen! No such luck. . .

Dad suddenly said, "I should think you could at least say good morning, Ernie." Mom mumbled something in my direction, then they continued hammering at each other. At least say good morning. . .as if I hadn't said it a dozen times already!

"The sooner the better," snapped Mom.

"Okay, okay," snorted Dad. "Just tell me when you'd like

11

to start. That is, if you really think you can do it!"

Dad should know better than to dare Mom that way. . .she might take him up on it, then where would he be. . .hey, where would we all be if they went through with this stupid idea? Oh, boy, I hope I am still dreaming.

"How's next week suit you?" Mom dared him right back with a glare.

I knew it, I knew it, Dad shouldn't have dared her!!

"Just fine. Dandy. Couldn't be a better time. Ernie will be started back to school by then and. . ."

"Wait a minute," I blurted. "Are you really. . .you can't really be serious about trading jobs, can you?"

"Well, I don't know about your father," sneered a very righteous Mom. "But I certainly am. I've been longing for some peace and quiet for ages now."

"I couldn't be more serious," said Dad, serenely.

"Me, too," added Mom, not one to let the last word go to Dad so easily.

Into this nightmare waddled Bitsey, half-carrying, half-dragging Claude, our cat. Perhaps I should mention here that Claude is rather a unique cat. . .a real individual among individualistic cats, with a personality all his own. Mom and Bitsey first saw Claude when they came to pick me up at school on a cold, rainy, November day. He was huddled in the corner of the school doorway, hoping somehow that he could scurry into a warm, dry place. His eyes and nose were running, and he was just generally a very bedraggled, miserable, sick cat. Even if Bitsey, the cat lover, hadn't carried on and insisted upon bringing "poor kitty" home, Mom would have, for she's a pushover for sick, helpless animals. . .a real softy. So she brought "that thing" as Dad insists on calling Claude, home and nursed him back to health. I said that as cats go, he is unique. Two things contribute to his uniqueness—his eyes, one blue, the other green—and the way he is marked by his color variations. Claude has a lot of white "fur," as Bitsey says, but half of his mouth is covered with a big splotch of yellow so that it looks like he has a permanent sneer on his face. Another attribute that keeps him from qualifying as a particularly stunning cat as far as handsomeness goes, is his boniness. No matter how much he is fed, no flesh seems to settle on his bony frame.

12

The last, and probably most outstanding of his characteristics, are his rather unusual habits, which I will describe to you in some detail later on. Now, back to the scene in the kitchen.

"Hi, Mommy. . .Hi, Daddy. .,.Hi, Ernie," said Bitsey through a yawn, looking at us with half-open eyes and a wide-open (as usual) mouth.

We all said good morning to her in turn. Boy, she sure knows how to get attention better than I do.

"Well, maybe I'd better take you down to the store this morning to begin to show you the ropes," said Dad in a very challenging manner.

Of course Mom picked up the challenge, as I knew she would.

"That will be just fine with me," she said sweetly. "As long as we save some time to come back here later in the afternoon so I can begin to orient you to these 'simple household chores,' as you call them."

"Daddy didn't say good morning to Claudie," whined Bitsey. The little creep didn't seem to understand that her entire world was about to be turned topsy-turvy.

Dad glanced at them out of the corner of his eye and, groaning a little as he always does when he looks at Claude, said, "Hi, Claude." Then, turning to Mom, said in a nicey-nicey tone of voice, "You'll have to brush up on your math, dear."

"Oh, boy," I thought. "He's really twisting the knife in now."

"My math is just fine, and furthermore. . ."

"Mommy didn't say good morning to poor, sweet Claudie, and Claudie's feelings are hurt," broke in the nuisance again.

"Morning, Claude. . .and furthermore," Mom continued in a voice every bit as nicey-nicey as Dad's, "If you have been able to handle it, it will be a breeze for me. I'm sure I'll have no trouble at all."

"Morning, Claude, " I said since I figured I would be next to do the honors, and, at that point, it was nice to have someone, even a cat, to speak to.

"Okay," said Dad. "Let's get going to the store." He sure was in a rush to get on with the disaster.

"Nobody kissed *pooooor* kitty good morning," whimpered

Bitsey. Claude was staring at all of us with an expression on his face which communicated absolute loathing, if not pure hatred. . .his normal regard for everyone except old Bitsey.

"Bitsey," warned Dad, who got his fill of Claude long ago when he woke up one morning and discovered Claude sharing his pillow, staring into Dad's brown eyes with his blue-green combination. Dad can't take a surprise like that first thing in the morning. "Bitsey," he repeated. "If you bring that thing any closer to me, I'll. . .I'll. . ."

"Put the cat outside, dear," advised Mom.

For once, Bitsey-bird-brain seemed to sense the mood in the room and this time didn't have to be told her usual number of times (as least three) before doing it. Out went a relieved Claude.

"Well, what are Bitsey and I supposed to do?" I asked indignantly. . ." Sit here and suffocate in Death Valley?"

"No, of course not," answered Mom. "Go get your swim suits and towels and we'll drop you off at the swimming pool."

"Mmmmmm. . .that doesn't sound so bad," I said. "Okay." I was thinking that even with Bitsey tagging along I would have plenty of time to swim with the gang after leaving her with the baby-sitters around the kiddie pool. I wouldn't really have to bother with her for the rest of the day. The day was beginning to look a lot more promising. . .it might just turn out to be a very nice day for me. . .that's all I knew. I would have had a better day if I had stayed at home and suffocated!!!!

CHAPTER THREE

Dad stopped the car at the entrance of the Pleasant Valley Community Swimming Pool, and Bitsey and I leaped out. Well, that's not exactly the way it happened. Bitsey, the little ding-bat, always has to have her "Lucky-Ducky Swim Ring" with her when she goes to the pool, and had slipped it over her shoulders in the car. Naturally, she wiggled and squirmed so much that it slipped down around her feet. She clambered out of the car first without tripping on it, but when I slid out, I some how got both of my feet inside the rim of that blasted ring. The minute that Bitsey moved forward, I fell flat on my you-know-what!

"Waaahhh!" creepo cried. "Mean old Ernie's trying to take Bitsey's Lucky-Ducky Swim Ring. Mommy, Daddy, make Ernie give me my ring!"

Mom sighed and said, "Haven't I had enough already this morning? Why do you have to be such a klutz, Ernie?"

Dad was shaking with laughter, "Oh, Ernie, you ought to see yourself. Ha, ha, ha!"

I stepped out of that stupid ring with all of the grace and dignity I could muster at that moment (which wasn't very much) and didn't say a word to anyone. Thank goodness, I would soon be rid of the pest and wouldn't have to worry about any more embarrassing situations for the rest of the day. . .I could just relax and cool off in the pool.

"Now take good care of Bitsey, keep an eye on her," instructed Mom for the hundredth time. "Make sure that she doesn't get near the deep pool, make sure that she's safely at the shallow one."

"I will. . .I will," I replied for the hundredth time. Boy, would I ever make sure that she didn't get near the deep pool where I would be. What a drag, trying to have some fun with your gang with a little creep to look after.

And, leaving us there, Mom and Dad drove off, taking the first step of a plan which would drastically change the lives of the entire Tubb family for the coming year. Little did I realize that the impact of my parents' job-trading would be felt so soon!

We had to stand in line to get into the dressing rooms, and Bitsey, already wearing her suit, pretended she was a

15

ballerina, holding that idiotic Lucky-Ducky Swim Ring around her waist, twirling and whirling on her toes, and bumping into some of the other kids who were also waiting in line. Of course I was the target of all of the dirty looks from them.

We finally made it in, and I laid our towels down on the bench.

"Gosh, it's hot," I said to Bitsey. "No wonder the pool is so crowded and we had to wait so long." I shoved the towels over and reached for my suit. . . suddenly, a sick lump formed in my stomach. . .for at that moment I realized I had forgotten to bring my suit! In my upset state over my parents' argument, and my hurry to get Bitsey into her suit, grab the towels, and not forget the swim ring, I had never given a thought to myself!

"Oh, no. . ." I cried.

"What's the matter with Ernie?" asked the little ballerina.

"It's my suit. . .I've forgotten my suit!"

"Poor Ernie. . .*pooooor* Ernie," crooned Bitsey. "Ernie should have worn her suit like Bitsey did."

"Ernie should have been born an orphan," I said, wondering what to do next.

"Ernie can call Mommy. Mommy will bring old forgetful Ernie's suit to the pool," smiled the little problem-solver.

"No, Ernie can't call Mommy. Mommy not home. Mommy already in bad mood. Mommy with Daddy at hardware store. Can't bother Mommy now," I explained in language I thought she just might understand.

At that very moment I had what I call an "Ernie special," a brilliant flash of thought. . .one which would solve my dilemma. I remembered that the Pleasant Valley Community Swimming Pool had "pleasant little suits" for rent. Boy, what a relief, just when I thought that this day which had begun so badly was going to get worse. Shoving Bitsey ahead of me, I hurried to the rent-a-suit counter.

"Can I help you, little girl?" asked a voice from behind the counter. It was a voice I recognized. . .it belonged to Doug Mitchell, who is only *one* year ahead of me in school. Boy, did that burn me up! He really had a lot of nerve to refer to me, Ernestine Cecelia Tubb, soon to be a sixth-grader, as a *little girl.*

16

"I am thinking of renting one of your "pleasant little suits," I murmured, assuming an air of sophistication.

"Yeh, Ernie forgot hers," butted in the big mouth.

"Ernie! Ernie!" sneered the disgusting twerp behind the counter, "You've got to be kidding! Ernie is a boy's name!"

"It just happens to be a nickname. . .short for Ernestine," I informed him in a very patient manner. "Now, could I please see one of your suits?"

"Gee. . .I don't think you'd like to see one of *my* suits even if you are called Ernie!" giggled the smart-aleck. He was laughing so hard over his little joke that he didn't notice the pool manager coming up behind him.

"Having trouble, Doug?" he asked.

Ha!. . .You should have seen funny-boy almost swallow his tongue. Boy, did he get busy looking for a suit.

"I'm afraid that this suit is the smallest we have left. . .big crowd today, you know," he said, with a sheepish grin.

"Fine. . .I'll take it, young man." Queen Elizabeth couldn't have said it with any more flair.

Well, back to the dressing room to change. I hadn't really looked at the suit at the counter, and so it was not until I began to put it on that I had an inkling that in addition to its being very large, it also was something of an antique. It was black and resembled something your grandmother might have worn fifty years ago. No, make it your great-grandmother and seventy-five years ago! It was really a dog. And, if that wasn't bad enough. . .imprinted across the front *and* back of the suit in large white letters were the words, "Property of P.V.C.S.P." I was mortified at the thought of being seen in this monstrosity of a suit, but being more hot than mortified, I decided to put it on. After all, once I was in the pool, no one would be able to tell what the suit was like.

I deposited the shrimp with the sitters at the baby pool and, with a sigh of relief that my troubles were now over, headed for the deep pool. But as I walked along I noticed that something strange seemed to be happening. . .my suit was twisting, turning, and bouncing in a very peculiar fashion. Not only did it twist, turn, and bounce whenever I took a step, the straps also kept slipping and sliding off my shoulders! I had to move very carefully and keep clutching at

17

the straps or else the entire suit would end up around my ankles, just like Bitsey's "Lucky-Ducky Swim Ring!" I couldn't think of anything else to do but keep on walking—step, step, step, twist, turn, bounce, clutch. . .step, step, bounce, turn, twist. My only hope was that I wouldn't meet anyone I knew until I was safely submerged in the water, or, if some of the kids were already there, they wouldn't recognize me in this get-up.

"Good grief, Ernie," called a voice. "Where did you get that suit?"

"Oh, hi, Louise," I gloomily replied. "Isn't it awful? But I forgot mine, and this one was the only rent-a-suit they had left." Louise was in my class at school last year and she and I were never really close friends. She's okay.

"Come on over to the other side of the pool. We're all over there. . .almost the whole gang. . .and we're having a great time," coaxed Louise.

That was just what I was afraid of. . .all of the kids *were* there, but I couldn't think of any way out, so off we went. What a picture we must have made: Louise in her smart, new pink and white polka-dot bikini and me, Ernestine, in my bounce-along, twisty-turny frogman's outfit! The only thing needed to complete the picture were flippers on my feet.

As we neared the other side, that dumb-head John Murphy let out a loud scream, ran behind two of the other kids, and shouted—mind you—shouted so the whole world could hear, "Help me. . .save me. . .somebody pu-leeze save me! It's the creature from the Black Lagoon!" Then he pretended to faint and fell backward into the pool. Good, I thought, I hope you sink right to the bottom and stay there forever. But of course, he didn't, and the next minute his head appeared at the edge of the pool with a big, repulsive grin on his silly face. Well. . .that's all the encouragement that was necessary to turn the boys into a mass of frightened, quivering, frenzied idiots, taking turns falling into the pool in fake faints! Fortunately, they soon tired of this activity and instead decided to start the game of "pearl diving." What this game is, is that Ralph always brings this round metal piece he has with him, and we take turns being the "pearl diver." Whose ever turn it is takes the silver piece, tosses it into the pool, then dives in after it. The object of the game is to retrieve the

18

metal piece before it reaches the bottom of the pool. Naturally we always played at the very deepest end of the pool.

"I'm first," hollered Ralph. Well, who could argue with Ralph? It was his "pearl."

"I'm next!"

"No, you're not! I am!"

"No, get out of my way, I'm after Ralph!"

"Third!"

"I said second first!"

"Just try it and see what happens!"

"I'm fourth!"

In all the commotion of choosing turns, I momentarily forgot about the sad condition of my swim suit. By the time I wound up being the third diver in line I became aware that one strap of the suit was twisted around my neck while the "Property of P.V.C.S.P." was situated under each arm. I felt like a disaster area, and rather resembled a licorice stick. Thank goodness for Louise, I don't know what I would have done without her. She was second in line and as we were waiting for Ralph to come up, she quickly helped me get straightened out. While she was at it she criss-crossed the straps, making them much tighter. At least I wouldn't have to worry that everytime I moved the rope, long straps would fall off my shoulders or wrap themselves around my neck and strangle me. Instead the top of the suit was bunched together and I looked like a balloony, bouncy, black bean bag on legs. . .and that was an *improvement*!

Ralph soon surfaced, successful at catching his "pearl" before it sank to the bottom. Louise was next.

"Somebody better give Louise a compass so she can find the pool without her glasses," shouted loud-mouth Murphy. "Hey, Ralph, better turn her in the right direction."

Louise turned very red, but cooly ignored his teasing as she walked to the edge of the pool and threw in the silver piece. She had a bit more trouble than Ralph, but still was able to retrieve it in time.

"Hey, Louise, that was great!" I yelled. She gave me a big smile as she handed me the "pearl."

"Look out! Stand back! Watch for the huge splash! Watch out for the backwash! Here comes the big whale!" cackled

Murphy. He just never lets up!

"Go on, Ernie, you can do it," encouraged Louise. It crossed my mind that she might be a better friend than I thought. She certainly came through when I needed help.

I reared back, gave the silver piece a good toss into the center of the pool and dove in. It was an extremely fine, graceful dive, if I might say so...one of my best. But it was in the middle of my dive, while I was still in mid-air, that I realized I was to be plagued with yet another problem. You see, when I flipped off the side of the pool, my oversized swim suit, tight around the legs, filled with air! I had become a human air-pocket! What happened next can probably qualify as the darkest moment in a procession of dark moments in the long life of Ernestine Cecelia Tubb. Have you already guessed? In case you haven't, let me relive that painful experience for you. Let me just say that right then and there, I became the first human bobber in history! There I was, at the mercy of that ungainly suit—head, arms, and legs moving in a frantic effort to propel myself downward into the water, trapped but kept floating by the bouyancy of the air in the suit. It was impossible to move in any direction—up, down, sideways, foreward or backward.

"Hey...hey...." began the creep who couldn't keep his mouth shut. "Your suit must be filled with corks. Hey, gang, look at old balloon britches!"

Well, there I was, threshing wildly in the water, desperately trying to squish the air out of the suit, ignore Murphy, and gain control of the situation. Finally, after what seemed like hours, I worked all of the air out—well, it came out in big, gurgling bubbles—to the accompaniment of giggling babbles from the side of the pool. Everyone...even Louise...was in hysterics. I dove to the bottom, found the silver piece, and quickly swam to the other edge of the pool...the opposite side, where I could be alone, away from all the laughter and wise-cracks. I guess I don't have to tell you how very upset I was...the sooner I got out of the pool the happier I would be, if I would ever again know any happiness. I swam to the ladder and pulled myself out, thinking that I would soon be rid of this infernal suit and my troubles with it. Well, are you ready for what happened next? You're not? You say what more could happen? Just listen...here's what happened next. As I emerged from the pool, that blasted suit filled up with water in the same way it had filled up with air! Yes. . .you've got the picture. There I stood at the edge of the pool clearly visible to everyone there! Guess whose voice came floating across the water? Of course, none other than John Murphy's—megaphone-mouth Murphy. Between hoots and howls I could hear him yelling, "Hey, everybody. . .hey. . .look at the black blimp!"

I was so mad and humiliated I couldn't see straight! I walked in a nightmarishly slow-motion kind of movement toward the baby pool, followed by derisive comments and convulsive laughter, and a stream of water oozing from my suit behind me. I grabbed a startled and unbelieving Bitsey by the arm and headed straight for the dressing rooms. Fortunately, by the time we got there, all of the water had drained from the suit, and I changed clothes in record time. I took the hideous thing back to the rent-a-suit counter and tried to slam it down, but it just gave one last big squish and doubled over. That was the way I felt too. And do you know. . .can you imagine. . .can you guess. . .what that drippy Doug Mitchell had the nerve to say to me? He said. . .what he said was. . .that he hoped that I had had a pleasant time down by the pool. . .a pleasant time down by the pool!!!

"Oh, yes," I answered, "another typical *pleasant* day in pleasant Pleasant Valley!"

Well, you can see what a devastating effect my parents' decision to trade jobs had already had on my life on the very first day.

But the year of madness was just beginning. . .

CHAPTER FOUR

Before I knew it September had arrived, bringing with it the first days and weeks of school. It didn't take long to settle into the dreary routine of class 6-B of the Pleasant Valley Elementary School. We were only three weeks into the new school year, but it seemed more like three months to me. But if there was dreary routineness in my school life, there certainly wasn't in my home life. Mom and Dad, still serious about their job trade, had not tired of this switch in roles as I had thought they would. Mom happily got up early and went off to the hardware store to take care of business while Dad stayed at home to take care of the family's needs—well, at least he was really trying to take care of them. They both appeared to be enjoying themselves very much in this situation which is more than can be said for Ernestine Cecelia Tubb. Even though for awhile it looked as if this job-trading idea might actually work out to be better for all of us, it wasn't long until a major catastrophe hit, and who was the unsuspecting victim of this catastrophe, you might ask. . .certainly not Ernie, you might say. Your worst fears are confirmed. . .yes indeed, the victim's name is Ernie!

The date of September twenty-third should be engraved on my tombstone to mark the day that I died. . .really died. . .died of shame, humiliation, and embarrassment! Even now, I cannot look back on that terrible day without a pang of mortification!

The first mistake I made that day was in getting out of bed, but then, that has been a lifelong habit of mine, so how was I to know any better this day? The second mistake I made was to get dressed, another lifelong habit of mine done, until now, without any unpleasant consequences. I'm not saying I shouldn't have worn any clothes to school, but appearing without anything on probably would have caused less of a commotion than what I wore did.

You see, the whole problem started when my well-meaning, hoping-to-please Dad put too much. . .no. . .let me begin at the beginning.

I woke up in my usual cheerful mood. I always feel very happy the instant I wake up, just like Dad. Mom and Bitsey are the champion grumps of all time from the minute they open their eyes until mid-morning—that's another reason why I thought Mom would get tired of running the store—such early hours. The sun was streaming in my bedroom window, casting a lovely, golden glow all over my room. I greeted the sun, "Good morning, Sun." I looked in the mirror, smiled at the happy person reflected there and said, "Good morning, Ernestine Cecelia Tubb. I have the feeling that today is going to be a golden day for you. I have the feeling that this day is going to be such a great, golden day that you will never forget it. It will be a day to live in your memory forever." Boy, as a fortune teller, I'm a total washout! Oh, I have always remembered that day, but absolutely *not* for its great goldenness. But let me tell you more about it.

I stepped to the closet, "Good morning, closet," I boomed. Throwing open the door with a flourish, I went on, "Good morning, clothes. Today is going to be Ernestine Cecelia Tubb's great, golden day. Which one of you shall I choose to share every golden moment of it with me?" I looked over my dresses and decided that this was not a dressy kind of day. Perhaps a pair of jeans might be right. No, I suddenly knew what would be exactly right. . .a skirt and sweater. But not just any old skirt and sweater. . .my golden plaid skirt and matching sweater, both the color of my great, golden day! Perfect. . .absolutely perfect!

"I choose. . .I CHOOSE YOU!" I shouted, pointing to the gold plaid skirt. "For you are gold. . .and I must wear gold on my golden, sun-shine day."

As I slipped the skirt off the hanger I noticed that it seemed to stick a little and I had to give it an extra tug. "Probably something sticky on the hanger," I thought to myself. Then I realized the skirt felt a little rough and stiff, not soft and velvety as it usually did. "Oh, well," I said to myself. "It will take more than this to spoil my golden day." I tossed the skirt on my bed and turned to get my sweater out of my dresser drawer. "You will look like a little ray of sunshine," I told myself. "Bringing light and laughter into everyone's life today!" Well, I was right in one respect—I certainly brought a lot of laughter into the lives of a lot of people that day.

When I turned around to my bed again, I couldn't

understand what had happened, for my skirt had not draped itself across the bed in the usual way after I give it a toss. Instead, it just kind of stuck up from the edge of the bed in a funny way. . .and it looked as stiff as a board! I walked over and picked it up gingerly, don't ask me why, I don't know except that I was too puzzled to pick it up in any other way.

Are you ready for what happened next? Well, let me tell you, neither was "ever-ready-for-anything" Ernie. I stood the skirt on end, *and* ready now? That beautiful, sunshiny, golden plaid skirt stayed right in that position! Just stayed right there as if I was still holding it, not moving one iota. And do you know what it looked like? It looked just exactly like a gold, plaid lampshade! "Oh," I thought, "that Dad. . .just for a joke, he's put a big piece of cardboard inside my skirt to make it stick up like that. He just wanted to make me laugh. What a funny man he is. What a relief!" Thus reassured, I picked up the skirt and put my hand inside to pull it out. It was at that moment that I began to feel darkness blotting out some of my great, goldeny, sunshiny day. . .for there was no cardboard, only the skirt, stiff and heavy!

"Dad. . .Dad!" I yelled as I flew down the stairs to the kitchen where I could hear Dad whistling away as he fixed breakfast.

"I'm right here in the kitchen, Ernie," he chided. "Not five blocks down the street." He chuckled over what he probably considered a clever response, as I burst through the doorway.

"Good morning, honey," he added.

I had no time nor thought of politeness and greetings.

"Dad, it's my skirt!" I blurted out.

"Oh, you noticed," he said with a pleased look on his face.

"Noticed. . .noticed. . .Dad, what did you do to it?"

"Not *it*, Ernie, *them*. What did I do to *them.*"

"Oh, for heaven's sakes, Dad. All right, what did you do to them?"

"I washed them. Yesterday I went through your entire closet and washed *all* of your dresses, skirts and jeans. A good job, if I do say so myself," was his triumphant reply.

"*All* of them? You washed *all* of them? You washed every one of my dresses, every one of my skirts, and every pair of jeans?"

25

"I knew you'd be pleased, Ernie. Your old Dad's pretty efficient, isn't he?"

"But Dad, my skirt is, at this very moment, standing straight up on my bed looking like an Indian teepee!"

"Well. . .maybe I did put a touch too much starch in them. . .but you know, I'm still learning about these things. Your mother explained that she always adds some starch to your clothes."

"Good grief! How much did you use? A gallon per skirt?"

"Now Ernie," explained Dad with that certain edge to his voice which means no arguing, "I said I am still learning. I expect you and your sister to cooperate and not complain when some little thing doesn't work out exactly right. So go get dressed. Besides, I'm sure the stiffness will work out of your skirt once you begin to walk around in it. Hurry up, breakfast is almost ready."

Well, I knew it was no use saying any more, so I did as I was told, and went back upstairs and got into my beautiful gold sweater and matching gold plaid lampshade.

I tried not to think about how stiff and heavy the skirt was, but it was difficult to move through the doorway with the skirt scraping against both sides of it at once. That was when I made my third mistake. . .leaving my room. I should have locked myself inside all day, not coming out once. Instead, I started walking down the hall toward the stairs. Suddenly I heard a strange noise. Scritch, scritch, scratch! I stopped. . .and the noise stopped too, "That's funny," I thought. "I'd better check on the Sleeping Beauty." I moved on, and the noise started again. . .scritch, scritch, scratch. I cracked open the door to Bitsey's room and stood waiting. . .the noise stopped again too. Bitsey had a stranglehold on Claude and was sound asleep. Claude glared at me resentfully for disturbing him, stretched, and rolled over, turning his back to me. I closed the door and began to move toward the stairs again. Scritch, scritch, scratch. "There it is again," I said to myself, "maybe it's coming from the bathroom."

As soon as I opened the bathroom door and stood listening, the noise stopped again too.

"That's weird," I thought. "Why would that noise stop every time I did?" Slowly a sick feeling swept over me. Oh, no. . .it couldn't be that! Not all day! Not all day in school! Any hope of enjoying my great, golden day vanished, replaced with gloom. . .for I then realized that the puzzling 'scritch, scritch, scratches' were made by my gold plaid lampshade whenever I took a step.

I slowly scritch, scritch, scratched my way downstairs. Dad was still whistling happily away in the kitchen, unaware that he had ruined his daughter's life. He was into the second chorus of "Happy Days Are Here Again," as I made my entrance.

"Have a seat, Ernie," he invited without looking at me. "Everything is ready to eat." I'll have to admit that under ordinary circumstances it's a lot more pleasant to be with Dad in the mornings than Mom—that was *one* good thing that had resulted from their great experiment.

I was in for another surprise when I tried to "have a seat."

I was willing to sit down, but my skirt wasn't. I made several useless attempts to sit at the table, then gave up and decided to eat my breadfast leaning against the counter top. Then I encountered another problem: my Indian teepee kept me from getting close enough to the counter to eat. Dad couldn't help but notice my difficulties, and said, "Don't worry, honey, it will be alright by the time you get to school."

Twenty-five scritch, scritch, scratchy minutes later when I arrived at school, I remembered Dad's prediction. I understand now where my lack of talent as a fortune teller came from. The walk had done nothing to soften my skirt. . .if anything, it had made it stiffer and noisier.

Fortunately the halls were crowded and alive with the usual noise and confusion, so no one noticed Ernestine Cecelia Tubb's sad condition. I was safe as long as the noise level remained high. I went directly to my classroom. Several of the kids and Ms. Fizz, our teacher, had already arrived. Ms. Fizz looked up from her desk and smiled her "Good morning" smile at me as I passed her. I very slowly scritched-scratched my way down the side of the room.

"How's Miss Pleasant Valley Community Swimming Pool, the bathing beauty of all time? Win any more swim suit contests lately, Ernie?" called a voice from across the room.

Guess who was in my room this year. . .yes, you're

absolutely right. None other than that one and only all-time big-mouth, John Murphy! Mammoth, megaphone-mouthed Murphy! I ignored him completely, concentrating on moving as quietly as I could to get to my seat. . .thank goodness, he sat clear across the room and couldn't hear me for the hall noise. I was wondering when he would ever stop teasing me about that horrible day at the swimming pool. I should have known that he would forget that as soon as he found something else to tease me about. Unhappily, this was going to take place sooner than I wanted it to.

I took very small steps, trying to glide along with a graceful kind of side-step, and a minimum amount of noise, but I noticed that Ms. Fizz, who has very sharp ears, was looking around with a puzzled expression on her face, and I knew she was trying to figure out where the sound was coming from.

"Made it," I thought with a sigh of relief as I reached my desk. But I still had a bit of maneuvering to do to sit down. It was almost like trying to mount a horse side-saddle. I had to use both hands to scrunch down my skirt, then quickly slide sideways into my seat. I felt a great deal of accomplishment when I actually succeeded in sitting down, the first time that morning! I glanced around and, thank goodness, no one was looking in my direction.

"Boy, safe at last, now I can just sit here until noon," I comforted myself. I hoped that my gold plaid lampshade might be transformed back into original shape by then. I was almost happy again. . .the day seemed to glow a little more golden now. . .now that I had successfully negotiated myself into the classroom. . .now that I had prevented another one of "Ernie's embarrassing moments" from happening. But I was far too confident, for at exactly 10:23 a.m., disaster struck! I remember the time clearly because I was looking at the clock to see how much longer I would have to wait until noon, when I heard Ms. Fizz's voice repeating my name.

"Ernestine. . .please pay attention. Look at the board instead of the clock. Now, come to the front of the room and work the next problem for us."

"Oh, no. . .no, I can't. I don't dare!" I screamed to myself. I thought quickly, "I'm sorry, Ms. Fizz," I said. "But I don't know how to work it."

"Don't be silly, of course you do, this is just review," was her reply.

I wildly tried to think of another excuse for not moving out of my seat, like a broken leg, sprained ankle, or a brain concussion, but I knew I couldn't fool Ms. Fizz. So, very slowly and carefully, I slid my way out into the aisle and stood up. CREEEEAAAAKKK!! My skirt snapped back into an Indian teepee. I heard a few snickers from the back of the room. Oh, how could this nightmare be happening to me, Ernestine Cecelia Tubb! No matter how slowly or how carefully I walked or in what direction, the room was filled with the sound of "scritch, scritch, scratch." Ms. Fizz swung around from the board and stared at me with unbelieving eyes. Every scritch was punctuated with a giggle, every scratch with a guffaw! I kept hoping that the floor would open up and I would completely disappear from sight. . .but. . .no. . .life was not to be that easy for me on my great, golden day. . .Hah! I thought then what a simpleton I had been that morning only a few hours earlier, raving like a maniac about my great, goldeny, sunshiny day. Worst of all, I had to walk right past the desk of broadcast-mouth Murphy. As I did, he said in a loud whisper, "Wow! Listen to old sandpaper legs!" By the time I reached the board the entire class was having a giggling fit.

"Class!" snapped Ms. Fizz. "I won't have this. Quiet! Ernestine, go ahead and work out your problem."

"Work out your problem. . ." Oh, if I only could. . .I'd love to work out my problem. I'd have Mom and Dad back where they belonged, where each of them knew what to do, then I wouldn't have to suffer through indignities like this. But, here I was at the board, in front of an almost hysterical class, every eye upon me, watching and waiting to see what might happen next.

"Quiet!" commanded Ms. Fizz again. The sudden hush that followed unnerved me even more. I picked up the chalk and started to write on the board. "Scritch," came from the side of the room. I wrote again. "Scratch!" from the same source. I didn't have to hear Ms. Fizz call his name to know who was making the sounds.

"John Murphy, put your head down!"

I began working again, but in my extremely nervous state, I dropped the chalk. I looked at the white piece of chalk lying on the floor, then I looked pleadingly at Ms. Fizz. . . surely she knew what would happen if she made me pick it up.

"Pick up the chalk, Ernestine," she said. "We can't waste any more time."

Pick up the chalk! Well, get ready now for you are about to learn of the most colossal embarrassment of the minute. . .hour. . .day. . .week. . .month. . .year! As I bent over to pick up the chalk, my skirt flipped up and turned wrong side out, just like an umbrella does, revealing something that I hadn't realized until that moment. . .in my hurry, worry, and concern about my clothes, I had forgotten to change my pajama shorts. And wouldn't you know it, not just any plain, old pajama shorts, oh, no, the ones that Grandma (who still thinks of me as a little girl) bought for me with pictures of cutsey-pie little bunnies munching away on big, orange carrots! One quick flash of comfort ran through my mind right then: John Murphy had had to put his head down and didn't see what I was wearing. I should have known better once more, for when I glanced at him after getting my chalk and the skirt smoothed right side out again, he was peeking at me through his fingers, shaking with laughter!

I'll never know how I managed to get through the rest of that day. I wouldn't have if it hadn't been for Louise and a few other sympathetic friends. When I got back to my desk there was a note from Murphy. He had writtten, "Hey, Ernie, you won't ever have to worry about being called carrot *top*!" Oh, the humiliation and shame! Now I ask you, would all of this have happened if my Dad had been at the hardware store where he belonged, and my Mom at home where she belonged? The answer is obvious.

Well, after that sensational incident life seemed to settle down for a little while, almost to the point of normalcy. . .at least for our family. That is, until Halloween. . .

30

CHAPTER FIVE

"Well, it's been a most pleasant afternoon, boys and girls," droned Ms. Fizz.

Now, who does she think she's kidding? We had just finished our Halloween class party and there she was, propped up against her desk looking as if she had just been through the final days of World War II. Her hair was limp, her clothes mussed up, her hand trembled, and her voice quavered slightly. She looked as if she would go straight to bed the minute she arrived home. I've noticed that our annual Halloween parties at school seem to have this effect on many of the teachers at the Pleasant Valley Elementary School.

"Now don't forget to watch out for cars tonight when you go trick-or-treating," she continued. The last bell of the school day was about to ring, and class 6-B was anxiously waiting to be dismissed.

"And remember to say 'thank you' for. . ." the bell interrupted her and she gasped a weak, "Class dismissed."

Chairs scraped, desk lids slammed, locker doors creaked and banged, voices rose above one another and general chaos developed. In other words, it was the typical end of another school day. . .only today was Halloween and therefore special, so there was an added touch of excitement in the air.

Louise and I were going to go out trick-or-treating together tonight. Even though Louise lives in the country, we have become very good friends since a disastrous day in my life: the tragedy at the swimming pool. We have many things in common, chief among them being our deep *hatred* of John Murphy.

"See you tonight at 7:30!" hollered Louise as she headed for the school bus.

"Come earlier if you can," I shouted back. "See if you can stay all night."

"I'll ask! I'll try!"

Our house isn't very far from the school, only about three and a half blocks, so I have a short walk, but sometimes it seems like three and a half miles. Today was one of those times. I was being followed by loud-mouth Murphy and two of his creepy friends again. Usually I plan to leave later than they do if I don't get a head start, but I had forgotten all

31

about them today in my excitement about Halloween. I was worried that Dad might not have been able to finish my costume for tonight. Mom had always taken care of it before, but she was too busy at the store to help this year. Besides, she told Dad it was up to him to make all of my costumes now. So that was that and here I was with Murphy right behind me, and he had what he always enjoys, an audience for his teasing.

"Hey guys, be quiet. Don't you see who's walking in front of us? Listen carefully while she moves and you might hear strange sounds. . .some very straaaaange sounds! It's old noisy legs in person!" teased the mouth.

Wouldn't you know it! I told you he never forgets anything. Memory like an elephant and a mouth the size of a whale.

"Hey, Tubby. . .been swimming lately?"

What did I just say? Like an elephant! Like a whale! I figured my best bet was to ignore him and walk on. But I should have known that the cavern-mouth wouldn't give up that easily.

"Hey, bubble-britches, is it true your father wears an apron?"

That did it! That was hitting below the belt. I couldn't maintain my air of indifference or control my temper any longer. I turned and said defiantly, "What's it to you, big-mouth?"

Well, of course, I had played right into his hands. I had done just what he wanted me to do. The three of them started prancing around on the sidewalk imitating my father.

"Oh, my! I'm getting so tired of all of this washing and scrubbing," whined Bruce.

"Oh, my! Look at all of this dust and dirt!" added Albert.

"Oh, my! Just look at my poor hands," mimicked megaphone-mouth, "I'm so worried about them being in water all of the time. They just don't look as nice as when I was doing my work at the hardware store!"

Then they all collapsed on each other, sprawling on the sidewalk in hilarious fits of laughter, just tickled to death at their own "cleverness." I whirled around and stalked off, shaking with anger, too angry to think of anything to say. Even after I turned the corner, I could still hear their heehawing.

"Bunch of drippy hyenas!" I muttered in a low voice.

It's impossible to have any secrets in Pleasant Valley so the kids (and their parents) soon found out about my parents' decision to exchange jobs. Some of them thought they could tease me about it, but I quickly squelched all of them. . .that is, except the unsquelchable creep, of course. A few of the kids, including Louise, were really envious of me and thought my parents were doing a fantastically marvelous thing. Evelyn even went so far as to use the descriptive word *brave!* But most of the kids (and from what Mom and Dad let drop, their parents too) thought it was stupid and silly, practically unnatural, and certainly un-American. I think by now you know what Ernestine Cecelia Tubb thinks about it. Let me just add that I hardly consider it a *brave* deed. . .the only one who has to be brave in this situation, this whole crazy situation is your very own long suffering Ernie.

As I turned into the driveway, I heard the other loudmouth sounding off.

"Kitty. . .kitty. . .kitty. . .kitty. . .here Claude. . .Claaauuude!" yelled Bitsey. "Claaauuude. . .Bitsey wants you. . .Claaauuude!. . .come to Bitsey!"

I hurried into the house to escape the noise. I really needed some peace and quiet by now.

"I'm home, Dad."

"Hi, Ernie. I'm in the kitchen," hollered Dad. I swear that's his favorite room, now. I slammed my books on the dining room table and went to find him.

"How was school today, honey?" he asked, offering me a freshly-baked cookie.

"Oh. . .school was fine," I said, between bites. "We had our Halloween party this afternoon, you know. It was fun, it was the walk home that was terrible."

"Murphy teasing you again?" Boy, one thing about Dad, he sure can zero in on a problem. "Well, just ignore him," he advised.

Just ignore him! If that wasn't a piece of useless advice. . .I had spent half of my life trying to ignore him! Trying to ignore Murphy was like trying to ignore the Marine Marching Band!

"Did you get my costume finished for tonight?" I asked changing the subject, almost afraid of his answer.

33

"Sure did, Ernie. You'll be the greatest looking nurse in town," he said proudly.

I raced upstairs to my room and there it was, lying on my bed. And you know—he had really done a terrific job—no starch in it at all! It looked every bit as good as the ones I've seen in shops.

"Thanks, Dad," I hollered down. "It looks fantastic!"

"Claude. . .come here, Claude. . .kitty. . .kitty. . .kitty!" Bitsey's piercing voice came through my bedroom window. "You bad kitty. . .come down right now. . .come down here to Bitsey!"

I walked over to the window and looked out, but I was entirely unprepared for what I saw. There, sitting on top. . .that's right, on top. . .on the very top of the garage roof, was Claude. He was wearing the most pathetic expression you've ever seen. We have a small white cupola in the center of the garage roof that looks like a miniature bell tower minus the bell, and that's where Claude was sitting—right in the middle of it. I raced down the stairs, yelling for Dad.

"Dad. . .Dad. . .it's Claude!"

"Claude, what about that infernal cat?" asked Dad as he bent over the oven.

"He's up on the garage roof sitting in the bell tower and he looks scared to death. He can't get down by himself, we've got to help him. If we don't get him down, he'll fall and hurt himself, or maybe he'll starve to death right up there on the roof with all of us watching! We've got to do something real fast. Oh, poor Claude. Come on, Dad."

You see, when I get excited I tend to rattle on a bit. I had said all of this without stopping to catch my breath, and while I was struggling for air, my Dad had the nerve to crack what he thought was a joke.

"Well," he said, "we've never had a bell in that tower so I guess it's only appropriate to have a ding-a-ling there instead."

"Dad. . .this is not funny," I said indignantly. "You've got to help us get him down."

"Now look, Ernie. . .I'm terribly busy right now finishing up the Halloween cookies and preparing dinner for all of you and I can't be bothered. Besides, cats are supposed to be able

34

to climb *down* as well as up. Just let the ding-a-ling go, he'll come *down* when he's hungry."

I could see that I wasn't going to get any help from Dad. Mom wouldn't be home for at least another hour, maybe later if she had had a busy day at the store. Boy, if she were only here, she could talk Claude down. Claude always did whatever she wanted him to. Oh, well. . .I just had to take matters into my own hands. I flew outside to check and sure enough, Claude was still up there, mewing in the most pitiful way you can imagine. Bitsey was close to tears.

"Oh, Ernie," she called. "Look at Claude. He's so scared. Help Bitsey get Claude to come down."

"Yes, Bitsey, I hear you. I see Claude. I will help Bitsey get Claude down," I humored the little creep.

We had loaned our long ladder to Louise's folks a few weeks ago, so I looked around for some things to stack on each other so that I could climb up on them and rescue that poor scared cat. There was a big barrel in the corner of the garage so I yelled for Bitsey to help me move it. The barrel was empty but still very heavy so we had to try rolling it. While Bitsey and I were struggling to move it, Chester, one of the neighborhood kids, appeared. Chester is seven years old and not too bright, if you ask me.

"Whatcha doing?" asked Chester.

"It's Claude. . .it's Claude," moaned Bitsey. "He's on the roof, in the bell tower."

"On the roof!" repeated Chester. "In the bell tower! What's he doing up there?"

I figured a stupid question deserved a stupid answer. So I said, "He's watching for the British."

"Has he seen any yet?" asked Chester.

See what I mean about not being too bright? Chester seems to be a little light on brain power.

"Oh forget it, Chester," I snapped. "Just help Bitsey and me move this barrel over to the side of the garage."

"Oh, now I get it," exclaimed Chester. "You're going to catch Claude in the barrel."

"Good grief, Chester," I exploded. "Don't try to think. . .you'll blow a fuse."

Evidently Chester followed my advice, for he stopped talking (and presumably thinking) and helped us move the

35

barrel. As soon as we got it on its end next to the garage wall, I told the two shrimps to search for other things we could stack on top of it. Within minutes Chester was back with three bricks and a large board. I discovered a large paint can and an old tire in back of the garage.

"Lookie, lookie what I got," sang Bitsey.

"Oh, Bitsey," I said, "Good for you." She was coming across the yard dragging half of a broken ladder.

We had placed the barrel open side down, stacked the bricks on top of it, then the can of paint, then the board, and, finally, the ladder. We propped the car tire against the barrel to keep it from slipping, hoping that it would hold steady. All of the time we were working we could hear,"Meow! Meow! Meeooow!" and that made us more frantic than ever.

"Hurry, Ernie," begged Bitsey. "Claudie is dying!"

"No, Bitsey, Claudie is not dying," I soothed her, but I was plenty worried about him myself.

"Do you think that stuff will hold you?" asked Chester, giving our stacked-up pile a questioning look.

"Of course it will," I said disgustedly. "Don't you know anything about aerodynamics?" I wasn't sure what aerodynamics was, but it certainly shut Chester up.

"Now. . .you and Bitsey will have to hold the barrel steady while I climb up," I directed. "For goodness sakes, don't let it wobble!" To be truthful, I wasn't too crazy about climbing on that stack of junk, but just then Claude gave another mournful "Meow!" and I knew I had to help him down.

As the two midgets took their places next to the barrel, I began the long climb up the junk. First up to the bricks that were on top of the barrel, then, very slowly, over the paint can to the board. I carefully moved one foot to the board, then the other to balance myself. Very cautiously I placed one foot on the first rung of the ladder. It shook a little and so did I.

"It's kind of wobbly up here," I shouted down as I gritted my teeth. "Can't you hold it any steadier?"

"We're doing the best we can," whined Chester. I could tell he was getting scared.

There was no answer from Bitsey. . .she was oblivious to *my* problems. Her entire attention was centered on "poor

Claudie's" plight. Over and over again, she kept saying, "poor Claudie. . .oh, poor, poor Claudie. . .Ernie's coming Claude. . .poooor, poooor kitty!"

As I climbed higher on the ladder I could feel the entire stack of junk begin to sway.

"Hold on tighter," I called down to my two incompetent helpers.

I had almost reached the level of the garage roof when I looked down. I immediately realized I shouldn't have done that, for a wave of dizziness swept over me.

"Boy, it sure looks high from up here," I yelled, again gritting my teeth.

"Don't look down," Chester ordered."You're making everything wiggle."

I could detect a note of concern if not downright panic in his voice. This made me feel even more insecure as I was depending upon him to help Bitsey hold the pile of junk together.

"Just a few more rungs. . .just a few more," I was telling myself. "Keep putting one foot after the other and soon you'll be high enough to rescue Claude."

"Ernie," yelled Chester.

"What?"

"Hurry up."

"Good grief, Chester, I am hurrying!"

"Hurry quicker."

"Why?"

"Because I have to go to the bathroom. Right now."

Naturally. Of course, Wouldn't you know it! This always happens to Chester whenever he gets excited and nervous.

"Try to wait," I yelled back. "Only one more rung to go, then I'll have Claude."

Slowly I moved up to the last rung of the ladder. As I raised myself up, my head became level with the garage roof and I was able to see Claude. I looked at him and softly called his name. "Claude," I coaxed. "Come to Ernie." He turned and looked at me with a look which registered halfway between terror and disgust.

"Here, Claudie. . .here, kitty," I whispered. "Come to Ernie, Claudie." Each time I spoke the barrel and everything that was balanced on top of it swayed and shook.

"Hurry up, Ernie, I can't wait much longer," shouted Chester.

That dopey kid! It would be my luck that he was the only kid in the block to come along when we needed help.

"Oh, poor kitty," repeated Bitsey. "Poor kitty...come down to Bitsey."

"Hurry, Ernie," Chester called once more. This time there was no concern in his voice—only panic!

"Claudie...nice kitty...come to Ernie," I pleaded.

Claude turned his head again, gave me a long stare, and slowly began to pick his way out of the bell tower, stepping carefully onto the garage roof. Cautiously, very cautiously, he crouched on the sloping roof, heading directly toward me. I held my breath. To this day I believe that my heroic rescue attempt would have worked out fine if that blasted car hadn't backfired at that exact moment.

Several things happened all at once, to create a disaster of enormous proportions:

(1) Claude's whiskers and tail went perfectly straight, his eyes widened, and he made a giant leap from the top of the roof to the top of my head.

(2) Bitsey and Chester both covered their ears with their hands, leaving no one holding the barrel.

(3) I grabbed for Claude as I saw him leaping through the air, thinking only of catching him before he fell to his death.....thereby taking both hands off the edge of the roof.

Due to these three things, the entire pile of junk crumbled and disintegrated from under me. The last thing I remember is hearing Chester yelling something about "can't wait any longer," over my screaming.

Then out of a greenish fog I vaguely remember seeing Dad's face looking at me through a round window. "That's strange," I thought, "We have no round windows in our house." Then I realized he wasn't looking through a window...he was peering at me through the opening of the barrel. Yes...that's right...Ernestine Cecelia Tubb had fallen off that junk pile and somehow managed to overturn the barrel and fall into it. There I was, looking like a canned tuna! Now I ask you...what else could go wrong? Wasn't it enough that a well-meaning girl landed in a barrel in this gone-wrong rescue? Well, more did go wrong. You remember that old can of paint that we used in our stack? It seems that the lid was just loose enough to come off when the pile fell apart, and now I not only looked like canned tuna, I looked like GREEN canned tuna. GREEN!

Dad pulled me out of the barrel and after he found out that I was okay, he was insensitive enough to stand there and laugh his head off.

"I'm sorry, Ernie," he wheezed. "But you should just see yourself!"

I looked around and through a greenish haze saw Bitsey cuddling Claude in her lap.

She was murmuring, "Poor Claude. . .oh, poooor Claudie. . .poor kitty. . .did that mean old Ernie scare you? Did mean old Ernie hurt you? Oh, poor kitty."

Claude turned and looked at me with the most smug expression imaginable, turned back to Bitsey, looked up at her, and began purring contentedly.

CHAPTER SIX

At seven o'clock that evening I was ready and waiting for
Louise to arrive. That is, as ready as I could be after many,
many unsuccessful attempts to remove the effects of the
unfortunate rescue incident. Poor Claude was just fine
now, but I was covered from head to toe with a tinge of
green from the *almost* empty paint can.

"Good grief!" exclaimed Louise as soon as she saw me.
"Whatever happened to you?"

"Oh, Louise," I answered with a sigh, "you wouldn't
believe it if I told you. Let's just say that I tried to do a brave
and heroic deed and ended up in the bottom of a barrel
swimming in a gallon of emerald green paint." Of course I
knew that this explanation would not satisfy Louise and I
would have to tell her the whole story. The whole *horrid*
story of how Claude was stranded on the roof, mewing
piteously, possibly even dying. . .of my daring and ingenious
effort to rescue almost accomplished. . .and finally, of pure,
unadulterated disaster. . .not leaving out any of the gruesome
details. By the time I finished my story, Louise was laughing
so hard she was almost in tears, hysterical tears. Well, I
suppose a person might be able to see a slight degree of
humor in my story if she wasn't turning black and blue under
the coat of green paint from the bruises and battering she had
suffered, but it's a bit much to go into hysterics. After Louise
calmed down, she tried to be sympathetic, but every so often
she would burst out in muffled giggles.

About this time, Mom came downstairs with a little fairy
princess walking in front of her. Who else? None other than
our little Miss Big-Mouth! The little creep was in a fairy
princess costume complete with magic wand. She was so
excited about being allowed to go out on Halloween that she
couldn't stand still, and had to keep crossing her legs.

"Hi, Louise," called Mom.

"Hi, Mrs. Tubb," answered Louise.

"Say, you really look great in that robot costume."

Louise had on a large box painted silver-gray which
covered her entire body. She had smaller boxes, the same
silver-gray, on her arms and legs, and on her head sat a box
with the front cut out. Her face was the same silver-gray as

41

the boxes. Antennae and wires stuck out of the box on her head.

"Ernie's green," helpfully pointed out the sweet little fairy princess.

Mom looked at me and said, "Well. . .we got some of it off anyway."

I walked over to the hall mirror and stared into it. "There's no doubt about it," I said. "I'll be the only GREEN nurse in the entire community of Pleasant Valley."

"Time to go tricky-tack. . .Bitsey wanna go tricky-tack!" screamed you-know-who.

"It's called trick-or-treat, honey," corrected Mom.

"I want to go!. . .I want to go!" continued the little Halloween terror, paying no attention to what Mom had just told her. "Tricky-tack. . .tricky-tack!"

Now, I have one question for you. Who had been chosen to take the little creep out to "tricky-tack"? Of course, the silver-gray robot and the emerald-green nurse.

"Oh, Bitsey," said Louise. "You look so cute in that darling little fairy princess costume." For some strange reason she has always seemed to take a special liking to Bitsey. "Can you cast any magic spells with you magic wand?"

"What's a magic bell?" asked the little word-scrambler.

"A magic *spell*, dopey. . .not bell," I groaned. "Don't you ever get anything right?"

"Of course she does," broke in Mom, giving me her "be nice to your sister or you'll be sorry" look. "A magic spell is when you tap someone with your magic wand, say a magic word like "shazam" and turn them into something else, like a toad or a lamppost."

It couldn't have been more than two seconds later that our dear, cute, intelligent little darling reached back and dealt a crashing blow to the silver-gray robot's leg while screaming, "SHAZAM. . . .YOU'RE A TOAD!"

Unfortunately, this was an indication of the way our evening was going to go. This was the first of many magic spells cast by the sweet and charming fairy princess in the course of her "tricky-tack" activities.

Dad came out of the kitchen with his camera in his hand.

"Wow, Louise, what an outfit," he said. "I want to get a

picture of you and Ernie together." He instructed us to stand close together and I noticed that Louise was limping a little, favoring her right leg where she had been smashed. Dad knelt on one knee and told us to smile and not look silly as he held the camera to his eye. Not look silly! How could an emerald-green nurse not look silly in a color slide? Just as he was about to take the picture, the fairy princess decided to work her magic a second time. Bitsey struck again with her magic wand. . .letting Dad have it right on the top of his head!

"SHAZAM!. . .YOU'RE A BIG, WOOLY BUG!" she shouted. Bitsey adores big, wooly bugs.

Dad was so stunned that he dropped his camera. Mom quickly hurried us out the front door, telling us to be careful and to come back early because of Bitsey. As she closed the door we could hear a roar coming from Dad.

We were no farther than the front steps when the fairy princess started whining, "Claudie. . .Claudie wants to come along. Claudie wanna go tricky-tack."

"No, Bitsey," I said firmly. "Claude wants to wait at home so you can show him all the things you get tonight. You can tell him all about your tricky-tacking." I had had enough of Bitsey and her Claudie that day already.

And so we went off down the sidewalk. . .one silver-gray, slightly-damaged, limping robot, one emerald-green nurse, and one deadly little fairy princess. Our parade moved rather slowly due to the robot, but we finally made it up to the first porch which had a light. It was old Mr. and Mrs. Robinson's house. The fairy princess flew up on the porch, hopped up and down, and screamed "tricky-tack. . .tricky-tack!" at the top of her voice. Mrs. Robinson came to the door with a basketful of chocolate bars.

"Well, well, well," she cooed. "Just look at the darling little girl on our front porch tonight. And what, may I ask, are you?"

Now right there is where Mrs. Robinson made a big mistake. You see, she should have never asked the magic fairy that question. No, what she should have done was to dole out her treats, slam the door shut, and count her blessings. But no, she had to ask Bitsey a question. Her answer was quick in coming.

"I'm a fairy princess. See my magic wand. I can make magic bells with it."

"Magic bells. Ha, Ha, isn't that cute!" oozed Mrs. Robinson.

Quick as a flash, before the silver-gray robot and the emerald-green nurse could even make it to the porch steps, the cute fairy took her magic wand and whapped the basket right out of Mrs. Robinson's hand. As the chocolate bars scattered all over the porch and yard, the princess screamed, "SHAZAM...YOU'RE A FAT WORM!" Bitsey also adores fat worms.

The magic bell-maker then bent over, scooped up several candy bars, turned and skipped off the porch, happy as a lark! Through all of this Mrs. Robinson could do nothing but stare at Bitsey in utter disbelief. I turned the robot around and we left as fast as possible.

"Hurry up, Louise," I urged.

"I am."

"We better be long gone before the shock wears off Mrs. Robinson."

I ran ahead and grabbed the fairy princess...the delicate princess with the deadly aim. By the time Louise caught up with us I had already threatened Bitsey that I would take her home immediately if she ever did that again.

Bitsey looked at me with wide-open, innocent eyes, and said,"But I was only making a magic bell. Mommy and Louise said that fairy princesses have to make magic bells."

"Well if this fairy princess makes any more magic bells tonight we'll never get any treats," I told her sternly. This seemed to settle her down, but you just never know with Bitsey.

The next house we came to was where the Hammers lived. All three of us trudged up the front steps. It took a bit of doing for Louise because of her bulky, rather unmanageable costume, in addition to her sore leg. Bitsey did her tricky-tack routine when Joe Hammer, who goes to high school, came to the door. He kept staring directly at me in a rather fascinated way while he handed each of us a popcorn ball.

"Say, Ernie," he finally asked with a puzzled look. "Do you feel all right?"

44

"Couldn't feel better!" I boomed as I whirled around preparing to shoot off the porch before he could ask any more questions. Just then Bitsey's voice broke through demanding a popcorn ball for Claude. "Claudie told me to bring him a popcorn ball."

"Who's Claude?" asked Joe. "Is he your brother? I didn't know you had a brother."

"Never mind," I interrupted, sweeping Bitsey off the porch with me. She ran on ahead of us, and as I was hurrying to catch up with her, I heard a loud thud followed by a muffled groan from behind me. I turned to find one silver-gray robot stretched out flat on the sidewalk. Evidently her visibility was hampered by the box on her head and she had missed one of the steps.

"Oh Louise, are you hurt?"

"No. . .at least I don't think so. . .but I can't get up. Help me up, Ernie, please."

We both struggled and for a while I thought we might have to call for a tow truck, but we finally got the robot on her feet once again. Maybe I should say "foot" since in her fall the boxes on her right leg, her injured one, had been torn off and smashed. In her fall she also had managed to land right square on top of her popcorn ball, which now looked like a popcorn pancake.

Floating to us from down the street were the sounds of "tricky-tack. . .tricky-tack," and we knew we needed to hurry to catch up with the little monster. Louise could move much faster now that she was minus one robot leg. But even with our hurrying, by the time we got to the Baldwin's front walk, the fairy princess was bolting off the porch. Poor Mr. Baldwin was just standing in the doorway with a very strange look on his face, rubbing his knee. The magic wand had struck again! I ran on ahead of Louise and grabbed the little wonder.

"Okay!" I loudly proclaimed. "That's it. You've done it now. You're going home this minute!"

Well, I expected a fight but not the Civil War! She screamed and kicked and stomped and jumped up and down. I was trying my best to control her while at the same time heading her in the direction of home, when suddenly I felt something give. I stiffened. I guess Bitsey could tell that a

45

disaster of unlimited dimensions had just occured because she became quiet immediately.

"Louise. . .Louise," I whispered. "Louise. . .the back of my dress. . .look. . .look at the back of my dress!"

Louise limped over to me and examined the disaster.

"Oh, Ernie!. . .oh. . .oh, my. . .oh, Ernie!"

"Stop saying 'oh, Ernie,' and tell me just how bad it is!" But I really didn't want to know.

"It's bad. . .real bad," said Louise. "Your dress has split right down the middle, all the way from the neck to the hem!"

"Oh, Louise. . .oh. . .oh, my. . .oh, Louise!" I thought that Dad had done such a great job. What could I do now?

Bitsey couldn't keep quiet any longer. "Bitsey will put a magic bell on Ernie. Bitsey will turn Ernie into a bumpkin."

"*Pumpkin*, not bumpkin. I already feel like a bumpkin, and don't you dare touch me with that awful magic wand!" I cried.

"Let's get you back to your house before anybody sees you," suggested Louise.

We were headed that way when out of the shadows we heard, "Hey, guys, look who they let out of their cages tonight."

Now wouldn't you know it! Who would be the last, the *very* last person on earth that I'd want to run into at this moment? Yes, you're right again. . .it was John Murphy. The mouth that knows all and tells even more. There he was, along with two of his friends, coming right towards us. My first instinct was to turn and run, but I quickly thought better of that, particularly the turning around part.

"Hey, Tubby! You look a little green. In fact, you look a whole lot green," roared the big-mouth. "Oh, I get it, guys. Tubby is dressed up to look like a Martian nurse! Then if she sees a sick flying saucer she can help it out."

"No, Murph, you're wrong," laughed Bruce. "I think she's dressed up to look like a caterpillar that can't make up its mind."

Albert also had to get in his two-cent's worth. "You guys are both wrong," he added, "Can't you see that she's a stalk of celery?"

I looked at Louise and she looked at me reflecting the

dismay and disgust I felt. Now how were we ever going to get away from these drips? Then I had a truly great idea. . .yes, a brilliant idea. . .a real " Ernie special"!

"Bitsey, dear," I purred. "Come and show the fellas how you make a magic bell with your little wand."

"What's a magic bell?" asked John, looking a little suspicious. He hadn't expected this kind of reaction to his teasing.

"That's what Bitsey calls a magic spell," I said smoothly. "Come on, Bitsey, show the boys what you can do with your magic wand."

"But Ernie," began Bitsey. "You said. . ."

"Never mind that now," I ordered. "If you want to do any more tricky-tacking do what Ernie tells you. Now!"

I turned back to Murphy. "Now, get down on your kness," I commanded.

"What kind of a dope do you think I am?" roared the mouth.

"Oh, are you afraid of a little girl and a magic spell?" I asked with an air of innocence. The other two began laughing and making wisecracks about the megaphone-mouth. I knew he couldn't take that.

"Shut up!" he yelled. "Of course I'm not afraid! Okay, where do you want me to get down for the magic *bell*?" he asked sarcastically.

"Oh, where you are will do just fine."

Murphy knelt and Bitsey walked over to him.

"Now Bitsey," I prodded, "I want you to cast the *biggest* magic spell you can. The *biggest* and *best* that you have ever done."

Boy, you should have seen those big eyes of hers light up! She looked straight at Murphy, who was now on her eye level, grabbed her magic wand with both hands and walloped him across the head so hard that she bent her magic wand! "SHAZAM!. . .YOU'RE A LIZARD!" she screamed. Then I grabbed her hand and the three of us tore off down the sidewalk at high speed. We didn't stop running until we reached our yard. We were out of breath so we just stopped and stood there, breathing hard. There we were: one slightly damaged silver-gray robot minus a leg, one emerald-green nurse whose costume had split, and one fairy princess with a broken wand.

From close by we heard the mournful meow of a cat.

"Claude!" cried Bitsey

"Claude," I agreed.

"It sounds like he's right above us," said Louise.

The three of us looked up in the trees. As we were looking, we heard another mournful meow, closer and clearer. It was strange. Where could Claude be if he wasn't in a tree? Then it hit me! I looked up at the garage roof. . .and yes. . .after everything I had gone through that afternoon to get that cat down. . .there he was. . .sitting in the bell tower again!

CHAPTER SEVEN

Three weeks before Thanksgiving, Mom, Dad, and I were sitting at the breakfast table, when Dad proudly announced, "We're going to have a real, old-fashioned Thanksgiving this year. None of those packaged foods for me. We'll have all naturally prepared foods just like the Indians and Pilgrims who celebrated our first Thanksgiving." I must tell you right here, that Dad has been buying those little food magazines that you see for sale at all of the food markets. He had obviously just finished reading an article on "an old-fashioned Thanksgiving" and was enthused with the idea. He was now in the process of planning our annual feast, and was determined that this, the first Thanksgiving meal he had ever cooked, would be the finest in the history of the Tubbs'.

"Today," he went on, "we will go buy a turkey."

"Food City usually has very good turkeys," volunteered Mom.

"Food City, *really!*" sneered Dad. "When I said we were going to have an old-fashioned Thanksgiving, I meant just that. *Everybody* knows that if you buy a *live* turkey you can feed and fatten it in just the proper way to make it the tenderest, most delicious bird ever to sit on your table." (This was probably on page 23 of his magazine.)

"You've got to be kidding!" exclaimed Mom. "A *live* turkey!"

"A *live* turkey, yessir, that's right. We're going to go out to Turkle's Turkey Farm this afternoon and get one. The Tubbs are going to have a hand-picked turkey for themselves this Thanksgiving. It will be a holiday dinner we'll always remember!"

Boy, was Dad right about that.

"In the house?" asked Mom. "You mean to keep a turkey in this house?"

"No, not in the house. In the basement. We have plenty of room for a little pen in the basement. We can get that at the turkey farm too," patiently explained Dad.

Mom didn't say anthing else then, but just looked at him like he had gone crazy.

I'll have to admit that I rather liked the idea. I could hardly wait to tell Louise. Bringing home a real, live turkey and keeping it in the basement sounded like a lot of fun. Boy, when I'm wrong, I'm really wrong! In fact, this was probably the most wrong I have ever been.

Mom left for the hardware store as usual, shaking her head a little every time she looked at Dad and thought about him getting a live turkey. Dad began cleaning up the breakfast dishes, so it was left to me to go upstairs and wake up Rip Van Winkle. Now that may sound like an easy job to you, but then you don't know what it takes to wake the grump up!

I ran upstairs and opened the door to Bitsey's room, to find her in her usual sleeping position. There she lay, feet on her pillow and her arms clutching Claude in a death grip. The covers were in piles on the floor all around her bed.

I pushed hard on the door and let it bang against the wall. Only Claude moved, turning his head, opening one eye, (the green one) then closing it again. Bitsey didn't respond at all.

I hollered, "Hey, Bitsey. . .time to rise and shine!"

Still no movement, still no answer.

Never one to give up, I trooped over to the bed and yelled right in her ear, "Bitsey. . .you've got to get up. . .Dad's taking us to the turkey farm." I thought that this bit of knowledge might be an incentive for the little creep to get up.

Claude opened an eye again (the blue one this time) but there were no other signs of life on the bed.

Well, in order to save time, I decided to immediately use my "sure-fire-Bitsey-wake-up" technique. This technique is carried out with the following actions:

1) Walk down the hall to the bathroom.
2) Fill one paper cup with cold water (the colder the better).
3) Hurry back to Bitsey's bedroom so as not to let the water temperature rise.
4) Stand next to Bitsey's bed.
5) Sprinkle small drops of the cold water on Bitsey's face.
6) Bitsey grumpily wakes up.

I very efficiently and quickly proceeded to carry out this "sure-fire-Bitsey-wake-up" technique—that is, through steps one, two, and three. Unfortunately, I never made it to step four which is "stand next to Bitsey's bed." For you see, as I was hurrying across the room, I accidentally got my feet all wrapped up in one of the little creep's blankets that she had deposited on the floor. So there I went, doing a first-class swan dive toward the bed! I must admit my aim was perfect, for I landed right on top of the sleeping princess *and* Claude. And, naturally, I managed to drench all three of us with what seemed like a gallon of water!

Screams, howls, yowls, and ear-splitting screeches brought Dad on the run.

"What on earth is the matter?" he yelled as he came through the door.

By this time, Claude was perched on the top shelf of Bitsey's closet looking like a drowned rat in the middle of a nervous breakdown. The queen hadn't moved an inch—but she was awake. She lay there, stiff as a board, eyes closed and screeching like a banshee as water dripped off her head onto the mattress. I had regained enough of my senses to lift myself off of the wild woman. There I sat. . .soggy and disbelieving.

Dad just stood there in the doorway in silence for about fifteen seconds, simply taking it all in. Then his face turned bright red, and he started laughing so hard that he had to sit down.

It was at this point that Ernestine Cecelia Tubb should have calmly gotten up, excused herself, walked straight to her room, closed the door, locked it, and crawled into bed for the rest of the day. But no, Ernestine Cecelia Tubb made the foolish assumption that the remainder of the day would be better because the worst had already happened. Well, believe me. I'll never make an assumption like that again.

Dad was still having fits of giggling every time he looked at me when we got into the car to go to Turkle's Turkey Farm. It had taken Bitsey and me a little while to dry off, and even longer for Bitsey to calm down after her morning surprise. Poor Claude was still a bit wet and shaking a lot. He kept twitching and looking around behind him every so often, as if he expected a repeat performance of his showering if he wasn't on the lookout.

Well, anyway, here we were in the car. Dad, Bitsey, me, and, regrettably, Claude. Dad and I were in the front seat, Bitsey in the back, and Claude lounging on the back window ledge.

"Daddy, can I have a chicken?" asked the little one in the back seat.

"Turkey, honey," explained Dad. "We're going to get a turkey for our Thanksgiving dinner. And the answer is no, if you're thinking about a turkey as a pet. We'll get one turkey and one turkey only—and that's the one we'll have for our great dinner."

"But, Daddy, I wanna turnkey!" she whined.

"Turkey. . .turkey. . .turkey!" I said, "It's pronounced *turkey*, not *turnkey*!"

"Daddy, why can't I have a turnkey?"

I give up! I bet the little creep will still be saying turnkey when she is a big creep.

"For one thing, Bitsey, we don't have any place to keep a turkey permanently. For another, turkeys do not make nice, clean pets for little girls," answered Dad.

"The turnkey could stay with me and Claude in my room." pleaded the never-give-up-trying-to-get-your-own-way-girl. "He could sleep with Claudie and me. Claudie would have a pet then too. The turnkey could be Claudie's pet!"

"Boy, wouldn't Claudie just love that," I thought to myself.

"Now look, Bitsey," said Dad with that edge to his voice, "I don't want to hear anymore about your having a pet turkey, or Claude having a pet turkey, or anyone getting one for a pet. It just wouldn't work."

Well, evidently Bitsey got the message because we didn't hear anymore from her except for some loud, deep sighs, until we turned into the lane which leads to Turkle's Turkey Farm. There must have been hundreds, even thousands, of turkeys in large pens strutting around eyeing us as we pulled into the parking area.

Bitsey let out a roar at her first sight of the turkeys.

"Turnkeys. . .turnkeys. . .turnkeys. . ." she wailed.

She was so excited that she bounded out of the car almost before Dad stopped it, and raced to the nearest pen. This caused a minor disturbance among the turkeys as they fluttered to move away from Bitsey. I figured right then and there that turkeys weren't as dumb as I had thought.

Dad jumped out of the car and hurried after the little demon.

"Bitsey, you're scaring the turnkeys, I mean turkeys," he said as he grabbed her hand and led her away from the fence. I was waiting for them at the doorway of the store when they arrived. Bitsey's eyes were as big as saucers and she kept repeating as if she were in a daze, "turnkeys, turnkeys, turnkeys."

"You can look at them again after we come out of the store," said Dad, trying hard to please the great "turnkey" lover.

There were a lot of other customers in the store, all of whom seemed to be ordering frozen turkeys, so it looked as if we were going to be there awhile. The "turnkey" kid perched herself on a window sill and kept her eyes glued to the turkey pens. Under her breath you could hear her continue murmuring, "turnkey, turnkey, here, turnkey, turnkey, come to Bitsey."

Dad gave me the nod that told me to keep an eye on Bitsey while he waited at the counter. Now, isn't that just like a parent! Me, Ernestine Cecelia Tubb, keep *my* eye on the little "turnkey" lover. She's not my little brat! But nevertheless, I had to forego my personal freedom to keep creepo from getting into trouble. I sat down next to her on the window ledge. She was still staring and murmuring, "Turnkey...here, turnkey."

"Well, here I am," I thought to myself. "Forced to stay with babble-mouth."

"Would you please be quiet?" I whispered to Bitsey. "People are beginning to look at you." I might just as well have been talking to the ceiling for all the good it did.

"Come here, turnkey...oh, pretty turnkey," she coaxed.

"Bitsey," I said a little louder. "Please stop talking to the turnkeys." I was furious but tried to keep a pleasant smile on my face since more and more people were looking over at us.

"Turnkey, turnkey, Claudie loves the turnkey."

"For heaven's sake," I muttered, while trying to look very busy picking lint off my pants. She was getting more and more excited, and subsequently becoming louder and louder.

"Turnkey, Claudie likes you, don't be afraid turnkey, don't run away from Claudie."

I was getting more and more embarrassed *and* I was running out of lint and patience!

"Bitsey, would you like to play 'I spy'?" I said, trying a diversionary tactic.

"Poor Claude, turnkey doesn't like Claude, poor Claude."

"I spy something blue," I continued.

"Claudie loves turnkeys, Claudie found a pet," said the little monster, getting louder and louder and still more excited.

Now, by this time, you know that I'm not one to give up easily, so I repeated, "I spy something blue and it's over by the counter."

"Ernie, Ernie, see how Claude loves the turnkeys."

"Okay, okay. Then will you play the game?" I tried bartering with her as I turned around to look out the window. I couldn't help what I did next. After all, what I had been through that morning, combined with what I now saw, was too much even for me to handle. I panicked! Do you know, can you guess what I saw at that moment? There was old Claude—right smack in the middle of all of those turkeys, hundreds of them squawking and fluttering, and trying to get away from our cat!

"Dad!!!" I screamed. "It's Claude, he's scaring the turnkeys out of their wits!"

I must have scared the daylights out of everyone there because for a few seconds there was complete and utter silence, except for Bitsey saying, "Claudie loves turnkeys." Then everyone began talking, yelling, and running toward the turkey pens all at once. By the time Bitsey, Dad, and I reached the pens where "poor Claude" was terrifying all of the turkeys, a man, probably Mr. Turkle, the owner, was entering it. He was trying to sneak up to Claude, very quietly and cautiously, and was just ready to grab him when Bitsey yelled in double high volume, "Claudie! Claudie!!" Claude took off with a giant leap and landed right on top of one of the biggest turkeys. You should have seen the horrified look on that turkey's face! You should have heard the commotion! All you could see was turkey feathers, dust, and the top half of Mr. Turkle! The noise was unbelievable. Out of all this choas walked Claude, as nonchalantly as if he was taking a stroll across our back yard. He slowly walked to the fence, leaped over it, and walked quietly back to our car. He then stepped into the car through the door Bitsey had forgotten to close in her excitement at seeing all the "turnkeys", curled up in the back window ledge, and lay there purring and watching the riot that was still going on full force in the turkey pen.

It took a while after Claude made his exit for the turkeys to settle down. Mr. Turkle and the remaining customers returned to the store, including Dad—but Bitsey and I were banished to the car. I was so embarrassed over the entire incident that I tried to disappear in the front seat but the little ding-bat thought it had all been great fun and was, in fact, quite proud of Claude.

"Oh, brave Claudie. . .Ernie, Claude found a turnkey friend. Claude is sooooo smart!"

Claude's purr became distinctly louder as if he was agreeing with everything Bitsey was saying about him.

"Maybe Daddy will bring Bitsey, Ernie and Claude back to the turnkey farm again next week, so Claude can find more friends." Bitsey just never knows when to stop.

Dad soon appeared at the doorway of the store carrying a crate. Out of the top of the crate, between two slats, bobbed the head of our turkey. Mr. Turkle followed him with a small pen.

"A turnkey. . .a turnkey," cried Bitsey. "Look, Claudie. . .our own turnkey."

Dad put the crate on the floor of the back seat, first warning Bitsey to keep Claude away from him. Dad's tone of voice told Bitsey she had better not mention a return trip—that it would be better if she didn't even talk on the way home. We began our long *silent* ride home. The only sounds to be heard were Bitsey cooing, "nice turnkey, nice Claudie," an occasional gobble, and some sniffing noises from Claude.

So, then, this was the beginning—the beginning of our memorable "old-fashioned" *real* Thanksgiving.

CHAPTER EIGHT

Well, the three weeks after the Bitsey-Claude-turnkey riot at Turkle's Turkey Farm passed in comparative calm. The turkey was put in the basement, living in comfort in the little pen Dad had bought at the turkey farm when we picked up our prospective "dinner". Bitsey must have made at least one hundred trips to the basement each day in order to "talk" to Toby. Yes, that's right, I said Toby. . .she named the turkey! You would have thought that Toby was her favorite playmate to hear their conversations together. She would stoop down on the floor beside his pen with Claude, the turkey lover, who would either be pacing back and forth in front of Toby's pen, or perched on top of it, swiping at Toby with one of his paws. (Claude's the kind of cat who always misses, though, when he's imitating the mighty hunter!)

"Hi, Toby," she would begin. "Wanna play today?"

"Gobble, gobble."

"What game would you like to play this time?" would be her next question.

"Meow, meow," would be Claude's comment.

"No, Toby gets to choose," was Bitsey's decision.

"What game, Toby?"

"Gobble, gobble, gobble, gobble, gobble, gobble, gobble!" came Toby's thoughtful answer.

"Oh, you'd like to play 'I spy,' okay," agreed Bitsey. Boy, did that burn me up! She wouldn't play with me at the turkey store.

"I spy something white," came the first clue.

"Gobble!" was the first guess.

"No, Toby, not the washer."

"Gobble, gobble," Toby guessed again.

"Meow."

"Now, Claude, don't laugh at Toby, or you'll have to go upstairs. Remember, he's just learning to play this game with us," admonished the little turkey-protector.

"Gobble!"

"Oh, Toby, you guessed it. It's Bitsey's socks. You're such a smart turnkey! Oh, Bitsey loves Toby."

"Gobble. . .gobble. . .gobble."

See what I mean? You would have thought that Toby was a human being the way Bitsey carried on. . .and a genius, at that!

I must admit, though, that I really enjoyed feeding Toby as long as I didn't let myself think why I was lavishing all that care on him. He was beginning to look very sleek and handsome, and each time I approached his pen I would feel like the witch in "Hansel and Gretel" as she was trying to fatten up Hansel. Toby would run to the side of his little pen when he saw me coming, stick his head out in my direction, and gobble like crazy.

As you may have already guessed, I, too, was getting rather attached to Toby during his stay with us. For a turkey, he had a lot of personality and appeal. But the way I felt about him was nothing, absolutely nothing, compared to the way Bitsey felt about him! Quite a close relationship had developed between her and our all-too-temporary house guest. Even though Dad kept telling us not to think of Toby as a pet because we were going to have him for Thanksgiving, it just didn't register with Bitsey. I guess it never occurred to her that her lively, feathered friend and companion-in-games would be our main course for our "old-fashioned" holiday feast. Whenever Dad told her we would have him for dinner she must have imagined Toby sitting in a chair next to hers at the dinner table with a big, white napkin tied around his neck, asking for another helping of mashed potatoes.

Yes, that's what Bitsey must have thought, right up to the time I arrived home from school on the afternoon before Thanksgiving. . .an unhappy day for Bitsey, but an even more unhappy one for Toby.

Bitsey met me at the door, with a stricken look on her face and big tears running down her cheeks.

"Ernie. . .oh, Ernie. . .hurry," she blurted out. "Help Toby. . .Daddy and Toby are fighting! Go help Toby!"

From the basement I could hear what Bitsey must have interpreted as a fight. "It was a fight; alright" I thought to myself "a fight to the finish. . .Toby's finish!"

"Gobble. . .gobble. ..squawk. . .gooobblle! screeched Toby."

"Come here, you *big, dumb turkey*!" yelled Dad.

The thuds, crashes, squawks, shouts, and other noises we

could hear indicated that a desperate chase was taking place.

"Hurry, Ernie," cried Bitsey. "Go help!" She ran across the living room and down the hall to the doorway to the basement. The little shrimp threw open the door, and we were both startled to see a terrified and bedraggled Toby come flying past her. His wings were flapping wildly, creating a trail of feathers streaming behind him as he came screeching through the hall. Dad was right in back of him. . .breathing hard, his face a deep scarlet, hollering words that I'm not supposed to know, let alone say. As soon as Bitsey saw them, she realized what Dad meant when he said we were having Toby for Thanksgiving dinner. She immediately began screaming, "No. . .let Toby go. . .let Toby alone. . .don't hurt Toby!" Sobbing loudly and hiccupping, she ran after them both, joining in the mad chase. The wild trio rushed into the dining room. I could hear gobbles, muttered threats, squawks, crying, more gobbles, mutterings, squawks, and crying. Then I heard a loud crash and an equally loud groan. As I ran to see what had happened, I was almost trampled by a crazed turkey fleeing the scene of the crime. Dad was sprawled out flat on the floor, surrounded by bits and pieces of Mom's favorite vase. Flowers were scattered all over the room, except for the ones clutched in Dad's right hand! Dad looked stunned, but not ready to give up yet. No. . .up he struggled, gave a glance around the room, uttered some indistinct words about "getting that turkey before he wrecks the house," and dashed off in the direction of the gobbles. You've got to say one thing for Dad, he's sure got spunk!

Then all of a sudden, the whole house became deathly quiet. I mean quiet. . .not a sound—no screams or sobs from Bitsey, no groans or shouts from Dad, and no gobbles or squawks from you-know-who. Just dead silence! "Well, Ernie," I said to myself, "the three of them have had a mass collision, and you will find them piled up in a big heap somewhere upstairs." I quickly ran upstairs to administer first-aid but was stopped suddenly by what I saw. No piled-up jumble of Dad, Toby, and Toby's friend and protector. No sign anywhere of Toby or Bitsey. There was only Dad, hunched over, peeking around the edge of my bedroom door. He very slowly and quietly crept inside the room and I crept in the same way right behind him. After all, if the action was going to start again in my room, I needed to be there to protect all of my precious possessions.

As I entered the room, I saw Dad on his hands and knees cautiously lifting the bedskirt. Claude leaped out at him, causing Dad to almost fall over backwards. Muttering something that sounded like "that blasted cat!" he straightened up and started tiptoeing over to my closet. He reached out his arm and flung open the door, just like the detectives on TV. With that simple gesture, the mad chase was on again, only this time it included an additional participant. That's right. . .Claude! When Dad flung open the door, both Bitsey and her turkey burst through the bedroom and ran into the hall. Unfortunately, the bed upon which Claude now reclined was in the path of the escapees, and Claude obviously felt compelled to join in the fun and games. There was quite a wild scramble for the hallway door, including a fantastic leap by Dad which took him sailing across the bed. Ernestine Cecelia Tubb just stood there, unable to comprehend the entire situation. The whole episode was from an old silent film, except that things were far from silent. Howls, gobbles, yowls, sobs, threats, screams, and more frantic gobbles seemed to be coming from every direction. Finally, a loud slam snapped me out of my daze and I rushed into the hallway myself. I was immediately covered by turkey feathers, bits of cat fur, and dust. . .I stumbled over one of Bitsey's shoes as I moved toward an ominously closed bathroom door. Coming from behind the closed door were more screams, gobbles, howls, and a few choice words from Dad. All of this noise came to an abrupt halt after a splash!. . .a rip!. . .and a thud!

Oh, no, I thought, what now? Am I the only living survivor? I cautiously opened the door. . .and there was Dad—draped over the bathtub with what was left of the shower curtain wrapped around him. Bitsey and her turkey were huddled together in one corner of the room. And Claude, you might ask, what had happened to Claude? Well, Claude's position took the cake! You will remember that the final sounds I heard were a splash, rip, and thud. Dad had taken care of the rip and thud, but it was Claude that had contributed the splash—yes, there was Claude peering out of the toilet bowl with surprise, chagrin, and yes, I do believe embarrassment written all over his little cat face!

It's hard to believe, but everything had settled down and was nearly back to normal when it was time to sit down and eat our Thanksgiving dinner. Bitsey and I had helped Dad to clear away the mess and straighten up the house before Mom got home. We even took time to replace her vase, so that she never could have guessed what had been going on while she was at the store. Dad had really cooked a delicious dinner and all of us, even Bitsey, were very hungry.

"Please pass the cranberry sauce," asked Mom.

"Dad," I said. "I'd like some more mashed potatoes, please." I looked over at Bitsey who was absolutely tearing into a turkey drumstick.

"Bitsey," I teased. "Do you really think you can eat that entire turkey leg?" Her mouth was too full, for once for her to answer, so she just nodded a vigorous yes.

"You know, honey," Mom said to Dad. "This is a great Thanksgiving dinner, better than any I've ever cooked."

Dad sat there with a proud grin on his face. "I told you the Tubbs' were going to have an old-fashioned holiday to remember this year," he boasted.

"Well, you were right," continued Mom. "Everything is just delicious, especially the turkey!"

"Yes," agreed Dad. "I know a good, tender turkey when I see it."

"You certainly do," said Mom. "But I told you that Food City has excellent turkeys. . .even if you can't buy them alive to fatten up yourself for your table."

Dad had no reply, but from down in the basement we could hear sporadic gobbles as Bitsey's reprieved "turnkey" ate his Thanksgiving mash.

CHAPTER NINE

We soon realized that Toby, our unexpected Thanksgiving *guest*, could not go on staying with us indefinitely, for a certain odor had begun to permeate the house. Dad solved the problem by contacting Turkle's Turkey Farm and convincing Mr. Turkle to take Toby back. I think that Mr. Turkle only agreed to do so on the condition that Dad, and only Dad, would be the one to return him. So, Dad made Bitsey believe that Toby was lonely and wanted to be with all of his old friends back at the farm. I wondered if any of Toby's old friends were still there, but I didn't say anything about that to the little turkey lover. Bitsey whined and whimpered about losing her turkey, but then one day when Dad was shopping, he found a turkey pillow—I'm not kidding—and she was all smiles again.

"Now I can take my turnkey to bed with me," gloated the little turkey-kid as she ran up to her room to find a place for Toby Junior, (naturally, she named it) and that was the last mention we ever heard of the real live bird. Even if Toby wasn't talked about, he was still remembered. How could any of us forget him! The basement and consequently the entire house smelled like Turkle's Turkey Farm! When Mom pointedly remarked about this smell one morning, Dad told her, "Don't worry, the basement will be all scrubbed out by the time you get home tonight."

"Good," said Mom. "Fine, it's way past time it was done."

I was really glad it was going to get cleaned too, until I glanced up and met Dad's glance and nod that clued me in on the fact that once again good old Ernie was being assigned another thrilling job...I got to clean up the mess in the basement.

I managed to avoid doing it for a couple of days through brilliant maneuvering and numerous excuses. But when Iris, a girl at school, asked me if I was wearing one of those new "back-to-nature" colognes that are on the market today I knew I'd better not postpone it any longer. I cleaned up the mess immediately after school that day!

The following Saturday was the Tubb family's reserved day for Christmas shopping. We were disappointed this year when Mom announced that she couldn't go with us, but had to stay at the store to check in a new shipment of Christmas gifts and toys. That left Dad, Bitsey, and me. Now you know that whenever this combination gets together, it is Ernestine Cecelia Tubb who has the honor of looking after the nuisance, so I was a little less than enthused over the idea of a whole day spent trying to control the Christmas kid. Dad had a list a mile long so I knew this would be an all day event. . .little did I realize just how *eventful* this day would be. We were driving over to the Miracle View Shopping Plaza so Dad wanted to get an early start.

"Hurry up, slow pokes!" hollered Dad as he waited in the downstairs hall.

"I am. . .I am!" I yelled back. "Boy," I thought to myself. "If *he* ever had to get the little creep into her snowsuit he'd be late too."

"Ernie, hurry Ernie," squealed Bitsey.

"Ernie's trying to. It would help if you would stop wiggling and hold still for a minute." Bitsey was so excited that she kept bobbing up and down.

"Bitsey's gonna see Sanie today. . .Sanie today. . .Sanie today. . ." she sang to herself. I figured if Sanie knew what was coming he would hide behind very large cartons in the stock room all day long.

"Bitsey! You're putting your arms in your leggings. Can't you help me a little?" I was getting madder by the minute.

"If you two don't step on it, we'll miss Christmas!" barked the patient father.

That's all it took to give the Christmas elf a case of the worries. Up she jumped, one leg in, one leg out of her leggings, and bounded and stumbled down the stairs, screaming, "Sanie!, Sanie. . .wait for Bitsey. Bitsey wants to see Sanie!"

Well, Dad and I together finally managed to contain the little dingbat long enough to get the snow suit on her. We were no sooner in the car, though, than she jumped out again calling, "Claude. . .Claude. .Claude, time to see Sanie!"

"Bitsey, get back in the car and stop calling that animal. You are never taking him in the car again." Dad was still angry over what Claude had done at the turkey farm. Bitsey could see that Dad really meant it, so she came back and got back into the car, and off we went—to the shopping plaza.

Big mouth sat in the back seat bouncing up and down and singing her mixed-up versions of Christmas songs all the way to the plaza. Her repertoire included "Jolly Old St. Frostee," "Rudolph, the Big, Red Christmas Tree," "Silent Night, Holes in the Night," and "We Three Kings of Oil and Tar." She was singing a nondescript song about Sanie coming down the chimney on his head when Dad turned the car into the parking area.

"Sanie. . .Sanie. . .Sanie!" screamed our little Christmas caroler. There, on the top of Waller's Department Store, was a huge display of Santa Claus being pulled in his sleigh by his army of reindeer. "I wanna talk to Sanie!. . .I wannna talk to Sanie!"

"Honey," Dad explained, "that's just a make-believe Santa. The real one is inside the store." I could tell by the expression on Bitsey's face that she fully expected to see a Santa of the same proportions inside, but I figured we could fight that battle when we came to it.

The plaza was packed with Christmas shoppers hurrying from store to store. Holiday decorations were everywhere and Bitsey's eyes were as wide as saucers. For once she just kept quiet and stared. . .she was entranced by the fairyland scenes all around her. Then from the center of the plaza we heard the high, shrill whistle of a train. Bitsey broke loose from my grip and bolted in that direction. Dad and I ran after her, dodging through the crowd, only to find her standing motionless and seemingly mesmerized next to "Santa's Express."

What Bitsey saw was a gleaming red and white engine pulling five long cars with seats just big enough for one person. All along the sides of the cars were painted scenes of Walt Disney characters playing in the snow. The train had just come to a halt in its picturesque little train station and dozens of little kids were getting off and walking out the exit ramp. As soon as the train was empty, another group of little kids ran to get on the "Santa Express."

"Me, too. . .me, too!" squealed our little Christmas angel.

"Why sure, Bitsey," said Dad, looking at me. "Ernie would be glad to take you on the train ride into Santaland."

"Bitsey's gonna ride a train. . .Bitsey's gonna ride a Sanie train," repeated the little twerp, over and over.

"Oh, boy," I thought to myself. "That's just what I want to do most of all." Dad bought the tickets and, noticing the look on my face said, "Now you know, Ernie, she's too little to go by herself."

"Oh, Dad," I wheedled. "I'm sure she could ride it by herself."

"Absolutely not!" was Dad's determined answer. "She's much too young for that."

I wanted to ask him why *he* didn't ride on the train with his little darling, but I thought better of it and simply resigned myself to a ride on the kiddie train.

"Here's two tickets," said Dad, handing them to me. "Now I want my two girls to have a good time riding into Santa's land."

I momentarily thought that I might throw up, but instead grabbed the tickets and followed along behind Bitsey into the entrance of "Santa's Express." The only two empty seats were the last two in the back. Bitsey ran and jumped into the very last seat, leaving me to struggle into the one in front of hers. Now when I say struggle, I mean to tell you that it was all I could do to try to fit into that stupid seat! I thought for awhile that I might have to hang my legs over the sides, but by crossing them Indian fashion, I managed to just barely squeeze into place. There I sat, feeling like a pretzel in a sardine can!

Then I heard a voice dripping with sweetness, saying, "I hope the wittle girl has fun on her wittle train ride into wittle Santa's land." I knew who it was before I looked up—that loud-mouthed, obnoxious John Murphy—and two of his drippy friends. Hundreds of people filled the shopping plaza, and it was my luck to run into them! I was mortified. I figured that the best defense was a silent one, so I ignored them in the hope that that would shut them up. I should have known better. . .nothing can keep the Murphy mouth shut. Not even Elmer's Super Glue!

"Maybe the wittle girl's mommy better go with the wittle girl," continued the drip.

"Yeh. . ." chimed in one of the others. "Her might get all scared and cry."

"If only the stupid train would start," I thought to myself.

"Ernie. . .make the train go," cried Bitsey.

Well, that was enough encouragement for the three baboons.

"Oh, Ernie. . .puleeze make the train go," mimicked one of the jerks.

"Don't worrry, guys, Ernie will make the train go!"

"Oh, but I don't think her can, cause her's so wittle."

By now, they were laughing so much that their words came in sputters, and they were leaning against one another to keep from falling down.

"No, guys. . .you've got it all wrong. . .it's the engine that's so wittle. . .I don't think it can pull that *great big, heavy* load!"

The big-mouth said the last four words very loudly. People standing around waiting for the kids were starting to laugh. I could feel my face turn red, and I prayed that the idiotic train would get going.

"Why, the little engine is going to have to strain to pull Ernie, the Elephant."

A whistle blew and the train finally started down the tracks. I could hear the idiots howling and laughing and calling, "I think I can, I think I can, I think I can," as we entered the tunnel into Santa's land. All of a sudden, everything became very quiet and *very,very* dark.

"It's awful dark in here, Ernie," whispered Bitsey in a shaky voice.

I figured I'd better talk to the little scaredy-cat or she might start crying, or worse yet, want to sit with me. The only way she could sit with me would be to perch on my head or shoulders, so I began a monologue which was to last through the entire train ride. Fortunately, the ride itself was rather short.

"It's always dark in tunnels," I began. "But pretty soon we will be out of the tunnel and into Santa's land. Bitsey will like Santa's land. Look up ahead. Oh, Bitsey, just look at those cute little elves riding on their little merry-go-round. They are Sanie's (good grief, now she has me saying it), I mean, Santa's helpers. Oh, and look over there. . .do you know who that is? That's Rudolph, your favorite reindeer, on top of that little house. I bet he's waiting for Santa to come up the chimney. Can you see Rudolph, Bitsey?"

I didn't hear an answer, so I figured the ding-bat was

either completely fascinated or still too scared to talk, so Ernie, the human pretzel, continued her travel guide routine.

"Bitsey. . .look over there, see, it's Santa's workshop. See all of the stuffed animals. Boy, there must be at least fifty different kinds of animals. I bet you would love to have Santa bring you one of those for Christmas, wouldn't you?"

Bitsey still didn't answer, although I heard a scuffling kind of noise which probably came from her twisting and turning in her seat to see everything I was pointing out to her. Good grief, I thought, it's like talking to yourself!

"Oh, Bitsey," I relentlessly continued. "Our ride is almost over. . .look ahead. . .you can see the opening at the end of the tunnel. We'll soon be back in the bright lights again." I thought this bit of news might cheer her up if she was still petrified with fear.

As we pulled out of the tunnel and into the little train station, guess who was standing at the railing waiting for us. Dad, you say? No. Wrong, *Very* wrong. It was the terrible threesome. I had momentarily forgotten they existed while concentrating on keeping Bitsey from crying.

"Here comes the Elephant Express!" yelled the mouth.

"Gee, I didn't think that little engine could pull such an *enormous* load," said one of the mouth's sidekicks.

"Hey, Tubby, you lost something!" shouted Murphy.

I decided to try ignoring them once again. "Come on, Bitsey," I said. "Let's get out of this place. . .the creepiness might be catching."

I untangled my legs and rather stiffly pulled myself out of my seat, then turned to pry the Christmas demon out of her seat. But the seat was empty!

"That's odd, " I thought. "How could she have gotten past me without my seeing her?"

"Little Bo-Peep lost her sheep, but Ernie's lost her sister and just looks sheepish," came a clever (he thought) remark from never-quiet John.

Looking around, I realized that Bitsey couldn't have walked to the exit ramp unseen. I figured she must have been more scared than I supposed and was hiding on the floor of the train car.

"Come on, now, Bitsey," I coaxed. "It's alright now," as I peered at the floor. At once, I felt the blood drain from my face and shivers shot up and down my spine. . .for the floor was empty. I was on the verge of tears as I turned to run and find Dad.

"Dad!" I wailed when I saw him walking towards me. "Bitsey. . .she. . .she's vanished!"

"Oh, come on, Ernie, she's just playing a trick on you," replied Dad. "Now go back and really look for her. We can't spend all day playing games."

Trying to check the tears and the panic, I ran back, calling "Bitsey. . .Bitsey. . .where are you, Bitsey?"

"What's the matter, dear?" asked the lady who sells the tickets at the train station.

"It's my sister. I can't find her!"

"Well, dear, where did you leave her?" she asked impatiently.

"Right there," I replied, pointing to the empty seat where she had been sitting. " She was right there when we went into the tunnel, but when we came out she was gone. Vanished." I couldn't hold back the tears any longer, they were streaming down my face when Dad came over.

"Bitsey!" he roared. "Bitsey!" I could tell that Dad was starting to panic too. This only made me feel more frightened, causing more tears.

"Bitsey!" yelled Dad.

"Bitsey!" called the ticket seller.

"Bitsey!" called the train engineer.

"Bitsey!" I screamed.

A chorus of BITSEY came thundering from old megaphone-mouth Murphy and his friends. For once I was glad John Murphy was around. There was no answer. Bitsey didn't appear. Again we all hollered for her. Then from far away we heard a faint voice echoing, "Bitsey. . .Bitsey."

"Good grief," said Dad, with relief. "She's in the tunnel!"

With that realization, Dad, the train engineer, and I all started running for the tunnel.

"It's all my fault," I kept saying to myself as we rushed into the darkness of the tunnel. "It's all my fault. She fell out of the car seat and is probably lying across the track, hurt and bleeding! Maybe she even has a broken leg!"

"Ouch!" moaned Dad as he ran into part of the tunnel's wall. We were getting deeper and deeper into the darkness

69

and Bitsey's voice was becoming louder. What I thought at first was moaning and groaning now sounded more like cooing and murmuring. It sounded almost as if she was saying, "Bitsey loves Toby...Bitsey loves Toby. .Toby...Toby."

"Oh, no," I thought. "She probably hit her head and is having hallucinations about her Thanksgiving turnkey."

As we rounded the last bend in the tunnel, the three of us were jolted into a shocked silence. There, in the midst of Santa's Workshop, sat Bitsey, holding a big stuffed turkey. She looked at us with a delighted grin on her face, and said, "Look, I found Toby...I found Toby living in Sanie's Bigtop. Toby loves Bitsey. Toby...Toby...Toby." She was just sitting there as if nothing unusual had happened. I had just made a complete fool of myself. I was now eligible for the fool-of-the-year award. I had acted like a colossal idiot in front of everybody, especially Murphy and Company, and she just sat there with a look of complete innocence. My life was disintegrating around me, and she had the nerve to say to me, "Come and give Toby a kiss, Ernie. . Toby loves you, too."

Dad picked up the little creep from the middle of the display and all four of us walked quietly down the pitch-dark tunnel. Down the tunnel toward the picturesque train station. Down the tunnel toward the little red and white engine. Down the tunnel toward the little train cars with their painted scenes of Disney characters playing happily in the snow. Down the tunnel toward the middle of the shopping plaza. But worst of all, down the tunnel toward John Murphy and his hysterical companions.

I wanted to die!

"Oh, poor Ernie," began Murphy. "Poor Ernie got so excited on her b-i-g train ride that she lost her sister. Poor wittle..."

Then he caught sight of Dad's angry face as he emerged from the tunnel and broke off in the middle of a sentence, and he and his crew left in a hurry.

"Ernie, it's obvious I can't trust you to look after Bitsey while I try to shop. We'll have to go home!" Dad was upset, not with the ding-bat, but with me, Ernestine Cecelia Tubb, doing my best to keep the creep out of trouble, going through hardship and humiliation to keep the creep out of trouble. Well, I guess I shouldn't have expected any thanks or gratitude for all of my efforts. I didn't argue because I really wanted to leave, to get away from the Murphy crowd, to go home and never think about it again. Bitsey, however, was another matter. One of the biggest thrills of Bitsey's life was riding on the escalators and she began whining right away. "Bitsey wants to go on the alligator. . .take Bitsey to the alligator." That kid never says anything right. Her whining did no good this time, though, for Dad, without another word, just shooed us out to the car. I thought it was good we were leaving, for several nearby shoppers began looking around nervously for the alligator.

Dad relaxed once we were out in the car, and said, "Ernie, how'd you like to help me make our Christmas cookies this afternoon? It would give us an early start on our Christmas baking."

"Sure," I said. "That sounds great." I really love to help Dad when he's working in the kitchen. So the rest of our "Christmas shopping" day was spent happily and without further incident right in our own kitchen.

CHAPTER TEN

Well, at least I had one thing to be thankful for after our ill-fated Christmas shopping trip. . .I didn't have to worry about being teased by big-mouth Murphy at school on Monday, for our Christmas holiday vacation had begun. Louise and I managed to spend some time together at her farm and for once I didn't have to drag the little Christmas creep along with me. It was heaven!

Before I knew what happened, December 18th had arrived and Christmas was less than one week away. Bitsey was absolutely beside herself with excitement and each day thought of another toy, plaything, or pet to add to her "Sanie list." Even the normally sluggish Claude seemed to catch the air of expectancy that prevailed throughout our house. He spent a lot of his time up on the garage roof within the protection of the cupola. He just sits there and looks all around the neighborhood. When he comes down. . .oh, yes, I forgot to tell you, we found out that Claude really can climb down all by himself. . .he and Bitsey have long conversations about what he sees from up there. One night at dinner Bitsey announced, "I know why Claude goes up on the roof so much."

"Oh, sure," I said. "I suppose you just asked him and he told you."

"That's right, Ernie," she continued. "Claude told me that he thinks his whole name is 'Sanie Claude,' and he's up there looking for his lame dears."

"Sanie Claude! Lame dears!" I snorted. "Can't you ever get anything right?"

Bitsey didn't even hear me for Mom and Dad were laughing so loudly that they drowned me out. They're still repeating it to their friends as one of "Bitsey's cute sayings." Well, I must admit, the kid has a lot of imagination.

Dad is very much like Bitsey at this time of the year. . .beside himself. . .even more so than Bitsey, though. He was all fired-up over the holiday season, and was bound and determined to provide us with another "old-fashioned" holiday. He must have bought the December issue of that food market magazine. You would think that his attempt at an "old-fashioned" Thanksgiving would have rather discouraged him from attempting an "old-fashioned" Christmas, but no, Dad doesn't give up that easily.

"Yes, sir," remarked Dad yesterday after dinner while he and I were cleaning up the dishes, "this year we're going to have a *live* Christmas tree. I'm sick and tired of that aluminum monstrosity that we have called a tree for the last few years."

"That aluminum monstrosity will look pretty good to you when you're faced with cleaning up the mess from a live tree," said Mom as she entered the kitchen.

"Mess," scoffed Dad. "Why, it's worth cleaning up a little mess to have a real 'old-fashioned' Christmas!"

"Oh, brother," returned Mom. "So you're back in the 'old-fashioned' holiday spirit again."

"And what's wrong with that? That's what we need a little more of around here."

"Well, I guess nothing is really wrong with it, as long as it doesn't involve another *live* turkey."

"There you go again. You'll never let me forget that stupid turkey, will you? Besides, we're having ham."

"Oh, well, then of course you won't get another live turkey. You'll have to get a pig!" chuckled Mom.

"Toby! Toby! Toby!" squealed Bitsey who was playing with her truck under the kitchen table.

"No, honey," purred Mom. "Toby can't come for Christmas dinner. Daddy learned his lesson at Thanksgiving."

"Bitsey wants Toby!" cried the little creep.

Dad shot a dirty look at Mom, then turned to Bitsey and said majestically, "Bitsey, this Christmas we're going to have something so great, so good, that you won't even think about Toby. This Christmas we are going out to Christmas Tree Acres and chop down our very own Christmas tree! How about that, baby?"

"Oh, no," groaned Mom. "Just make sure you pick a time when I'm at the store."

Bitsey looked puzzled as if she wasn't sure this event could take the place of having her Toby back again.

To me, it sounded like fun. . .but then you'll recall that I also thought getting a live turkey would be fun!

Dad chose the next day for our great Christmas tree adventure pilgrimage. For once, probably in the spirit of

Christmas, he got the wiggle-worm dressed himself. I got the axe for him and waited by the car.

"Well, we're all ready!" said Dad, coming down the steps. Bitsey had on so many layers of clothes that she looked as wide as she was tall. "The Tubbs are on their way to chop down their very own Christmas tree."

"Chop, chop," echoed Bitsey. Bitsey really fell in love with the word. It was all we heard throughout our entire car ride. As she tired of saying it, then she put it into a song, "There be a chop time in the old town tonight," being her favorite. She kept alternating between the two until I was beginning to feel slightly mad by the time our car pulled into the snow-covered drive of Christmas Tree Acres.

As we crunched to a halt, Santa Claus, that's right, I said Santa Claus, came bounding out of the barn and over to our car.

"Ho, ho, ho. Welcome to Christmas Tree Acres!" he said as he half-pulled Dad from the car while shaking his hand. Bitsey scrambled out and I followed. Jolly old St. Nick's costume was so bad that even Bitsey wasn't fooled into thinking she was really seeing "Sanie Claus." He showed us into the barn where he gave us a long sled and some rope, then directed us toward the trees, telling us to have a "ho, ho, ho," wonderful time finding our tree, a wonderful time cutting our tree, and a wonderful time bringing in our tree. . .and, "ho, ho, ho don't forget to stop and pay for your *very own* tree!" So off we went, Dad carrying the axe, Bitsey trailing the rope, and me dragging the long, heavy sled.

We couldn't have gone more than twelve steps before the ding-bat started to whine, "Bitsey wants to ride! Put Bitsey on the sled! Ride!. . .Ride!. . .Ride!"

"That's a good idea," agreed Dad.

"I have a much better idea," I quickly countered. "Let's leave Bitsey in the barn!"

"Ernie!" warned Dad.

"Okay. . .okay," I said. "Waddle over here and plant yourself on the sled."

"Ride, ride, ride," sang Bitsey as she clumped through the snow and plopped her royal highness on the sled. And in that fashion the Tubb family continued going forward on the snow-covered trail in their quest for a Christmas tree to

75

surpass all Christmas trees.

"Keep a sharp eye out, girls, for the best-looking tree of them all. No little scrubby tree for the Tubbs this year!"

We went on and on. Every time I pointed out a tree that looked good to me, Dad saw some fault in it. Just as I thought my arms were about to become permanently damaged from pulling the Snow Queen, Dad shouted, "That's it! That's the tree for us!"

"Where?" I asked, stopping in my tracks.

"That tree," said Dad pointing to a very tall, well-developed spruce. "That tree will be the perfect tree for our very own."

"Christree. Christree," repeated the Snow Queen as she stepped down from her throne. "Chop, chop the Christree."

"Boy, Dad," I said, "That sure is a big one. Do you think we can get it into our house?"

"Of course!" he said. "Ernie, why don't you use your head?"

Use my head! Asking me, Ernestine Cecelia Tubb to use my head! Bro-ther! If I had used my head in the first place I wouldn't be along on this crazy hunt for a Christmas tree. After all, the parents of the other kids I know simply go out and buy a pre-cut tree. But no, the Tubbs have to be different. They have to trudge for miles through knee deep snow just to have an "old-fashioned" Christmas. But then, the other kids have normal parents who live in a normal way and do normal things. Many nights I lie awake wondering how I, Ernestine Cecelia Tubb, ever got stuck with such a mixed-up family.

"Stand back, girls," ordered Dad. "I don't want you in my line of fire."

Let me tell you that when Dad cuts down a tree, he doesn't waste any time. It seemed as if he had just begun when his call of "TIMBER!" rang across Christmas Tree Acres. Bitsey moved a little closer to me as the large tree began to tilt.

"TIMBER!" she shrieked in my ear as the tree came crashing to the ground.

"Well, girls," said Dad proudly, "that's how the early pioneers had to get their Christmas trees."

I thought we might be in for a history lesson but then he

76

said, "Now all that we have to do is get the tree back to our car."

"We should have borrowed a truck," I told him.

"Don't be silly, Ernie, we won't have any trouble fitting this tree on our car at all. Can't you be sensible?"

Right then and there I should have dug a large hole in the snow, climbed in and immediately covered it over so no one could ever tell I was there. You might say. . .but, Ernie, you would get all full of snow and cold and wet. HA!! Let me tell you that I could have gone swimming in the North Atlantic in the month of January and not gotten half as cold and wet as I did in trying to get that stupid "old-fashioned" tree back to our car.

Dad wound the rope around the tree, then tied it to the wooden slats of the sled. It was too big for the sled and hung over in all directions. Dad tested his tying job by shaking the tree from side to side.

"It doesn't look very steady," I said as the tree wobbled precariously on the sled.

"Oh, it'll hold," Dad assured me. "Ernie, I want you to walk along beside the sled and help keep the tree steady and balanced as I pull it back along the trail."

"Well now," I thought to myself, "that doesn't sound half bad." I had figured that I probably would have to be hitched to the front of the sled like a team of oxen and pull the whole thing, including the little creep, down the trail by myself.

"Bitsey wanna ride. . .Bitsey wanna ride!" began the chatter-box.

"Okay, honey," agreed Dad. He set her on the trunk of the tree between two large bottom branches. She clutched the branches with both mittened hands, threw out her chin, and looked for all the world like George Washington must have as he led his troops into battle.

The tree started pitching back and forth the minute Dad began to move it. I twisted the rope around my arm to get a better grip on it as we trudged along back to the barn. Bitsey was letting out squeals of joy, but my arm was becoming numb from the constant struggle to keep the stupid tree steady.

I was just about to holler out to Dad for a rest stop when

it happened. Evidently Dad thought the stump in our path was just a big clump of snow because he pulled the sled right into it. The left runner hit it square on and the impact violently tipped the sled in the opposite direction from which I was standing. Now you will remember that I had wrapped the rope around my arm to steady the tree better. Therefore, as the sled and tree rolled over, my arm(and the rest of me) was pulled right along with them. Yes, that's right. . .good old Ernie became an unwilling living Christmas tree ornament. But not for long! You see, the sled and tree stopped only momentarily, then continued to roll right into a deep snow bank with the sled on top and the tree on the bottom. Well, that's almost accurate. The tree was really in the middle and I, Ernestine Cecelia Tubb, had become the base for our *very own* "old-fashioned" Christmas tree.

Far off in the distance I could hear the muffled voice of Dad yelling my name, and the muted screaming of Bitsey. People's voices sound really strange when your head is stuck in a snow bank and your ears are packed full of snow. I tried to yell back but it's quite difficult to make oneself heard when there's a branch of blue spruce stuck in your mouth. So I just gave up. I just lay there thinking of how wonderful it was going to be to have an "old-fashioned" Christmas when and *if* I was ever dug out of the snow bank.

It wasn't long until I felt Dad's hand grab my arm and I was hoisted out of the snow prison and back into the world of air once more.

"Ernie. . .honey. . .are you all right?" he asked with a worried look on his face.

"I geth tho," I managed to say through a mouthful of the tree.

He then hurried over to Bitsey who was sitting on top of my snow bank and screaming as if she was dying. Obviously she had been thrown clear of the Christmas tree death trap but was still too scared to move. . .except for her mouth! Dad finally quieted her down, then came back and helped brush the snow and bits of blue spruce off of me. That is, the snow and bits of blue spruce that were clinging to the *outside* of my clothes. I was soon to discover that I had scooped up a major portion of the snow bank *inside* of my coat and boots.

We repeated the whole process of tying the tree to the sled and this time managed to get it to the car without further incident. I might add that the Snow Queen was content to walk the rest of the way and never said another word about "ride!. . .ride!. . .ride!"

The tree was larger than Dad had thought and wouldn't fit into our trunk, so he and the jolly "ho, ho, ho" Santa Claus had to tie it to the top of the car. I resisted the impulse to tell Dad, "I told you so," and just got into the car. By the time they had the tree securely (I hoped) tied on, I was beginning to feel bits of the snow bank running slowly down my back while chunks of melting ice slid down into my boots. That was nothing though, compared to the waterfall that began once the car warmed up on the ride home. Dad knew I was quickly turning into "Miss Soggy Mess" (he could see the puddle on the floor) so he began to drive a little faster.

"I'll have you home in no time, Ernie. Then you can get out of those wet things and take a hot bath and. . ." his voice trailed off as he made a sudden stop to avoid hitting a car which pulled out right in front of us.

"Idiot driver!" Dad yelled.

As we stopped I heard an odd scratching sound on the top of the car and then everything went green! At first I thought I was seeing things until Dad let out a few more words that I can't repeat, then I knew his world had turned green too. Well, it seems as if old "ho, ho, ho" Santa Claus was not very good at securing trees to cars because now we had our *very own* Christmas tree as our *very own* hood ornament. I sloshed out of the car and helped Dad push the tree back onto the top of the car where it belonged while Bitsey waved and sang to all the people who had stopped to watch the sight. With my luck it figured that John Murphy would walk by and begin showering us with wisecracks, but for once he was nowhere in sight.

After this experience Dad drove more slowly. I guess he thought his precious Christmas tree was more important than his oldest daughter's danger of coming down with pneumonia. I was quickly growing to despise our "old-fashioned" Christmas tree.

As soon as our hurried dinner was over we began

preparations for decorating "it." Mom brought out several boxes of decorations from the closet while Dad mounted the tree on the stand. He was bringing "it" in the back door when he got stuck. . .simply wedged in!

"Hey, Ernie," he hollered. "I need some help!"

I'm sure you can understand that I was in no hurry to ever see that tree again after my experience with it that afternoon, but then Dad had that tone in his voice that told me I had better get a move on, so I hurried to the kitchen.

"Coming," I yelled.

"Hurry up!" called Dad as I entered the room. It was easy to see why he was so impatient. The tree was half inside and half outside and Dad was somewhere in-between.

"Ernie, grab a hold of the trunk and pull," he ordered. "We seem to be stuck."

"Okay," I said, looking for a good place to get hold of "it." Finding one I tugged in the direction of the dining room. . .but nothing happened. I said, "I think it's really stuck, I can't budge it."

"Well for heaven's sake, Ernie. . .try again," he ordered, raising his voice a little.

Old workhorse Ernie grabbed hold again, gave a hard tug, then another, but "it" seemed to have a mind of its own.

"Gee. . .I think that's really a unique place to put the tree, dear, I kind of like it, but don't you think it might be a little inconvenient to have the back door barricaded during the holiday season?" needled Mom as she came into the kitchen.

"Very funny," Dad replied.

"Claudie see the Christree. Look, Claudie," sang the little twerp as she dragged a bewildered-looking Claude into the kitchen. Claude arched his back at the sight of the tree and for once I agreed with him.

"Ernie," came Dad's order. "When I count three I want you to pull with all your might."

"One."

"One," echoed Bitsey.

"Two."

"Two," continued little Miss Echo.

"THREE!" shouted Dad as he gave a tremendous shove while at the same time I pushed as hard as I could. The force that Dad and I created together was more than we had anticipated and the three of us, Dad, "it," and I, went charging across the kitchen and into the dining room. We rather resembled the early Vikings storming a castle wall with a battering ram. In-between shouts from Mom, groans from Dad, sounds of branches scraping along the wall, hitting and knocking things over, I could hear a delighted Bitsey say, "Oh, Claudie. . .look. . .a choo-choo Christree!"

Dad and I managed to stop and stood in the middle of the dining room while Mom checked for damages.

"Well. . .by some strange miracle you two didn't break anything," said Mom. I could have told her that I thought my back was broken but knew she'd only laugh and tell me to stop exaggerating.

"Do you think the two of you could get that darling 'old-fashioned' tree into the living room without any further incidents?" she sarcastically continued.

Dad showed much restraint (or else he was out of breath like me) and simply barked, "Move it, Ernie!"

No one cared if my back was breaking or that my arms were being pulled out of their sockets. . .oh, no. . .just a "Move it, Ernie!" So Ernie, the slave, struggled through the archway into the living room and over to the empty corner that had been made ready for our five-ton Christmas tree. I began to think of our old aluminum tree with love. Dad and I were able to get the tree into an upright position without too much trouble.

"Pretty, pretty Christree," sang the ding-bat, dancing around the living room holding a disgusted Claude. "Claudie loves the Christree."

"Well, now!" said Dad triumphantly, "isn't she a beauty! It sure beats that scrawny silver thing we used to call a tree. And just smell. It really smells like Christmas."

"Claudie smell. . .smell the Christree, Claudie," instructed the midget as she thrust Claude's head toward the branches.

"Get that cat away from the tree, Bitsey," commanded Dad.

"Claudie wants to smell," whined Bitsey with big eyes.

"Claudie does smell," returned Dad, who then proceeded to giggle at his own cleverness which had simply gone right over the head of Claudie's owner.

"Well, let's get on with the decorating," said Mom, taking

some ornaments out of one of the boxes.

"Boy, it even looks bigger in here than I thought it would when you chopped it down," I said, trying to figure out where to begin decorating.

Now when I say big, I don't mean ordinary big. . .no, I mean super-big. It took us the entire evening to cover our outsized giant with ornaments, lights, and tinsel. Mom ran back to the store to get two more strings of lights and Dad had to bring in our stepladder in order to decorate the top branches, but finally the last piece of tinsel had been draped in place and the tree-top ornament, a beautiful glass bird, placed at the very top which nearly touched the ceiling. Dad told Mom to turn off all the lamps in the room as he plugged in the twinkling lights which covered the tree.

"Oh. . .it's beautiful," I said proudly. Maybe it was worth breaking your back for a tree like this.

"Yes, it really is," agreed Mom.

Bitsey just stood there with her mouth open, as if she was in a trance.

With a pleased look on his face, Dad walked over to where we all stood. "Now isn't this worth a little mess?" he asked Mom. Never one to give up, Mom responded, "It is as long as you're the one who's cleaning it up."

Dad ignored her remark and. . .are you ready for this? He actually reached out and joined hands with Mom and me and began to sing the Christmas carol, "Oh, Christmas Tree."

"Oh, brother," I thought. "Dad has gone all the way with this 'old-fashioned' business. Still, it was kind of nice. Mom and I joined in and after the first chorus Dad hollered for Bitsey to stop searching for that crazy Claude and come join us."

"But Claudie wants to sing about the tree, too," whined the creep, but she took hold of Mom's free hand and we all forgot about Claude. . .temporarily.

Into the second verse and chorus plunged the Tubb family. We were singing up a storm and beginning the third verse when I noticed the Christmas tree wiggle a little. That's right. . .I said wiggle. I thought maybe I was just seeing things after such an exciting day, so I continued with the song. But before we could finish that verse the tree wiggled again, this time more violently. The Tubb family singers stopped singing and simply stood staring in disbelief as a cat's paw emerged from the branches at the top of the tree! As we watched, the paw made a mighty swipe at the bird on top.

"Claudie!" squealed Bitsey.

Claudie, indeed. . .it was our dear, sweet, near-sighted Claude making an attack on the tree's bird. He lunged again, missed again, nearly fell off the tree. He panicked, and in an attempt to regain his balance, began scrambling around clutching at different branches. Ornaments and tinsel went flying! All of this was simply too much for the tree-stand to handle, and our beautiful, huge, "old-fashioned" Christmas tree came crashing to the floor, Claude and all!

Dad let out a roar, "If I can catch that cat, I'll kill him!"

Bitsey let out a terrified scream, "It wasn't his fault. The bird fooled him!"

Claude untangled himself from the branches, leaped over the broken ornaments and fled from the room, leaving a trail of tinsel behind him. Bitsey ran after him.

Mom rushed back to the store and gathered up armloads of new decorations and lights, while Dad and his workhorse cleaned up the mess, and we started the whole procedure all over again, with one exception. Bitsey was put to bed, and Claude put out in shame and disgrace. When we finished this time, there was no joyous singing, we were far too exhausted. And, instead of our beautiful glass tree-top bird, there was a little tin star at the top of the tree.

So began another "old-fashioned" holiday for the Tubbs.

CHAPTER ELEVEN

It was the middle of January, a month which, so far, had seemed bland and uneventful after our one-in-a-million "old-fashioned" Christmas celebration. I was looking forward to Friday, for we had a day off from school because the teachers were having a workshop day, and so I decided to call Louise to see if we could think of something exciting to do that day. Her line was busy so I wandered into the living room where Mom and Dad were talking. They were in the middle of a discussion of how best to take care of the annual inventory at Tubb's Hardware Store.

"Well, I always closed down the store for at least one day," said Dad.

"That sounds like a good idea," responded Mom. "I'm also considering having a pre-inventory sale this Saturday. Do you think that's too short notice? Today's Monday. . .that would give us four days to get organized."

"Plenty of time," said Dad. "You'll need some extra help, though. I'll come down and help one day."

"Oh, no you won't," said Mom. "We made a bargain and we're keeping it. . .you take care of things at home, and I take care of things at the store."

"Good grief," I thought to myself, "here it is January and we're still stuck with that stupid bargain they made way last August." I was surprised, truly surprised, and really chagrined that it had lasted this long. . .especially with all of the disasters we'd been having. . .well, the disasters I'd been having, because of them. Some of the kids at school were teasing me about my crazy family, notably that stupid jerk John Murphy, but things in the neighborhood had quieted down. I guess all the neighbors had finally accepted my parents' strange style of living. Well, let me tell you right now that Ernestine Cecelia Tubb had not, would not, could not, and furthermore never planned at any time in the future to accept it!

My preoccupied attention immediately was called back to my parents' conversation when I heard my name mentioned.

"Oh, I doubt if Ernie is old enough," Dad was saying. "I don't think she could handle that much responsibility."

"Nonsense," said Mom, "of course she is. She would be a

big help during the sale. There are many things she could do to help out besides waiting on customers."

Wow! Was I hearing right? Did Mom really say she wanted me to help out at the store? Was she actually going to let me work there a whole, entire, complete day? Wow! Before she could change her mind, I blurted out, "Oh, Mom, could I. . .could I? I'd work real hard and not get in anyone's way. You'd be proud of me. Could I, Mom. . .could I?"

"Why of course you can, Ernie," replied Mom, smiling in my direction. "You will be a big help. And you have Friday off from school, so you can come and help me *two* days."

Two days. . .oh, boy! I was beginning to have second thoughts about my resistance to our unusual family arrangement. After all, Dad had never asked for my help at the store. In fact, he always acted like I would just be a bother when I practically begged him to let me come down and help him. I decided that Mom was an excellent judge of character. . .much more so than Dad. At long last, Ernestine Cecelia Tubb was beginning to receive her deserved and due respect.

I was so excited Thursday night that I could hardly sleep. I kept having visions of the name of our store reading Mrs.Tubb and Daughter, instead of the Tubb Hardware Store. I could forsee a great future for me among the nuts and bolts. Mom didn't have to call me Friday morning. . .I was up and dressed, ready to go by the time she came downstairs for coffee.

"Settle down, Ernie," she told me. "You've been to the store hundreds of times before."

"I know, Mom," I said. "But never to work there!"

When we got to the store, Mom showed me what I would be doing. Besides just generally helping out, my main responsibility was to keep the shelves and tables filled with sale items. This meant that whenever I noticed a practically empty space I was to go to the stock room and bring out more of that sale item. Besides having a large stockroom in the back of the store, much of our stock was stored high along one side of the store on shelves. There was an attached movable ladder that could be wheeled along the entire length of the store in order to reach the many items on the shelves.

I stayed at the store all day helping Mom and the two salesmen, Joe and Art, get everything ready for the next day. Mom and I took a half-hour off to go out to lunch. . .she said I was such a good worker I deserved a break. Dad never appreciated the way I worked for him like that. By the end of the day I felt as though I knew every square inch of the store and stock room. I was also very tired. I must have gone up and down that stupid ladder a hundred times looking for one thing or another. But in doing this, I learned a little trick which not only saved wear and tear on my legs, but also saved time. Let me give you an example of how it works. Say I was on the ladder getting a steam iron off the shelves at one end of the store and I also needed a box of three-way light bulbs which are kept on the top shelf at the other end of the store. Well, before I had my "Ernie special" flash of thought, I would have to climb down the ladder, push it all the way to the back of the store, then climb back up to reach the light bulbs. But then my brilliant idea came. . .why bother climbing down? Why not just give myself and the ladder a little shove and *roll* from one end of the store to the other as I needed to? And so, with a slight push I found that I could propel myself along the shelves and stop at any item I wanted to get. As I said, this saved both time and energy. Yes, I was on the way to a promising career in hardware. By the end of the day I was getting quite good at it, if I do say so myself.

That night at dinner, Mom told Dad how quickly I seemed to catch on at the store. "Like mother, like daughter, I guess," she said.

At this point, Bitsey chimed in, "Bitsey wants to go help Ernie in the rock room. . .Bitsey could be a rock girl too."

"Not rock. . .stock," I told the word-scrambler. "And you can't come along."

"Bitsey wants to go," whimpered the creep.

"No, Bitsey," soothed Dad. "If you went along who would be here to take care of Daddy and Claudie?"

Bitsey didn't care what kind of job she had, so she settled down and didn't make any more fuss.

The next day Mom and I got to the store extra early to see to last minute details, as Mom put it. She was a little nervous and so was I. Joe and Art arrived a little later and soon we were ready. . .not only ready for the rush of customers, but also ready for the debut of Ernestine Cecelia Tubb into the world of commerce and business. It's a good thing I was there, because by ten o'clock in the morning many of the sale items had all but disappeared. From then on, it took all of my time just running for stock to refill the shelves and tables with those wanted sale items. By lunch time I was famished, but there was no time to go out today, so I just gulped down a tuna fish sandwich in record time while perched on my ladder and continued with my restocking. I was real pleased, and I know Mom was too, when several of the customers told her how proud she must be to have such an accomplished daughter.

"Oh, yes," I responded. "I think I may follow in my Mom's footsteps."

"Hey, Ernie," Joe hollered. "Would you please see if we have any more of those small cuckoo clocks?"

"Sure," I yelled back, and glided the ladder toward the middle of the store. The clocks were not where I thought they should be, then I remembered that they were much nearer the front of the store. I was just about to give myself a push on the ladder when a voice floated up from somewhere below me. . .a voice I not only recognized, but also had learned to hate.

"Well, look at that. Tubby's practicing to be a fireman."

Yes. . .it was the all-time loud-mouth, John Murphy. . .right here in the store. . .back in my life again.

"Hey, Tubby, where's your fire hose?"

I refused to look down or acknowledge his presence in any way. I simply gave the ladder a push and went rolling away from him toward the cuckoo clocks. Boy, did that ever shut him up! Out of the corner of my eye I could see the idiot standing there with a very surprised look on his face. . .with a touch of envy mixed in. He obviously never expected to see me ride down the side of the store on a ladder. "Well, congratulations, Ernestine," I thought to myself. "That's one for you, and none for Murphy."

"Ernie," called Joe again. "Did you find those cuckoo clocks yet?"

"Not yet," I answered. "But I'm getting closer."

In my haste to get away from Murphy, the mighty mouth, I pushed the ladder in the wrong direction. I had no alternative but to push back the other way. But that was all right because I would roll past him again and make his eyes bug out! And, so with an extra touch of the old Ernestine flair, I pushed off in the other direction. I was rolling along smoothly when suddenly I noticed a foot, to be more specific, John Murphy's foot, stuck out in the path of my oncoming ladder. There was nothing I could do to stop then, so I grabbed tightly to the top of the ladder and waited for the impact. I was half jerked off when it hit the imbecile's foot. Both of my feet flew off the rung and I was swinging wildly from side to side, hanging on now by one arm, and scrambling to get at least one foot back on the ladder when a high falsetto voice came from low behind a counter saying, "Fly home to your nest, you big cuckoo bird!" At the same time his arm shot out and gave the ladder such a push in the opposite direction that I lost my balance completely. I slid almost the length of the ladder before I was able to catch hold of one of the rungs, but by then was completely turned around so that I was behind the ladder, between it and the shelves, facing Mom, Art, Joe, Murphy, and all of the customers, all of whom were staring up at me in amazement. There I was, barrelling down the length of the store backwards, holding onto the ladder with one hand, and screaming, HELP! Before any help could come though, the ladder reached the end of its track and, along with me, crashed into the back wall with a resounding THUD!! The impact was so great that many of the stock items were knocked to the floor. . .along with me and my hopes for a bright future working with Mom in the store. As I sat there, too dazed to move or speak, one of the little cuckoo clocks I'd been hunting for fell off the shelf and landed on my head. The little bird's head bobbed up and down and a very faint "cuckoo, cuckoo" could be heard.

Mom and the customers came running over. "Are you hurt, Ernie?" she cried anxiously.

Before I could answer I heard the sound of a cuckoo calling from somewhere out on the sidewalk.

Score two for the big-mouth!

It took us a good part of the afternoon to properly replace everything that had come crashing down along with yours truly. I was totally embarrassed. . .just when I was trying to impress Mom with my responsibleness. She didn't yell at me, but I could tell she was very upset because I had made extra work for everyone, in addition to creating such a commotion in front of the customers. She knew I felt bad though, and on the way home said, "Ernie, I don't think we need to mention your little accident to your father. We'll just keep that to ourselves. Okay?"

"Oh, yeah. . .sure. . .okay. Thanks, Mom."

When we got home we were met at the door by Bitsey, who asked, "Did you have a good time rocking at the store, Ernie?"

I didn't bother to answer her and was on my way upstairs to lie down when Dad appeared in the kitchen doorway and said, "Well, Ernie, I hear there was a little excitement at the store today. I've had several people call me asking about your possible talent as a trapeze artist. . .or perhaps in a balancing act for the circus!" I might have known. . .in a small place like pleasant little Pleasant Valley, there are no secrets. Well, at least Mom meant well, and she defended me by saying, "Under the circumstances, Ernie did very well today."

But Dad just kept on laughing. . .at least he didn't say "I told you so," but then he didn't have to, we could read it in his eyes.

CHAPTER TWELVE

The rest of January passed swiftly, my days at school punctuated by a dreary tedium of work, and frequent calls of "cuckoo...cuckoo," whenever Murphy the ladder-mover crossed my path. I looked forward to Saturdays with joy and relief. I loved to sleep in but today I was rudely awakened, *very* rudely awakened...

"It's snowing...it's snowing," squealed Bitsey, running into my room, pouncing on the bed, then bouncing up and down on it. Boy, if there's anything I really despise it's being jolted awake by Bitsey the Bouncer.

"Look out and see the snow. It's snowing lots and lots," bubbled the little snow-flakey.

"Oh, goodie, goodie," I responded sarcastically as I put the pillow over my head.

"But Ernie...Daddy said he's going to take us tobobeling!"

I slowly lifted the edge of the pillow, "Where is Dad taking us?" I asked.

"He's taking us tobobeling!"

"I never heard of a place called 'Bobeling'...why would Dad want to take us there?" I sleepily inquired.

Bitsey jumped off the bed and stamped her foot. "No, no, Ernie...tobobeling!"

I tell you there are times when you need a code expert to decipher some of Bitsey's messages, but I didn't even think that would help this time.

I completely removed the pillow, sat up in bed, stared straight at crazy-mouth and told her, "Now Bitsey, say it again but say it very slowly and as clearly as you possibly can."

Bitsey's face took on a look of determination as she slowly began her sentence. "D-a-d-d-y i-s t-a-k-i-n-g u-s t-o-b-o-b-e-l-i-n-g ."

Still staring at her, I asked if she knew where Dad was going to take us tobobeling.

With the same look of concentration, she answered, "We will go tobobeling down the hill." She was beginning to get a little angry with me for not understanding her...isn't that a switch!

"Bitsey," I said, "do you, could you, mean that Dad is taking us tobogganing?"

"Yes. . .that's just what I said. . .why can't you understand?" she asked with a puzzled look on her face. "Today Daddy's gonna take Bitsey and Ernie tobobeling!"

I laid back down again and covered my head with the pillow once more now that the riddle from the mystery-mouth had been solved. I thought that might encourage her to go away and let me alone.

"Well," I thought to myself, "sledding has always been one of the things that Mom did with us, but I suppose Dad has taken over this one as well." I could never remember his going with us at all. . .he was always too busy at the store. Well, I guess it's true that there's always a first time for everything.

Instead of going away and leaving me in peace as I had hoped, Bitsey had jumped back on my bed bouncing to the rhythm of her made-up song. "Tobobeling we will go, tobobeling we will go, hi ho the fairy-o, tobebeling we will go!"

"What's the use?" I asked myself. I decided that Saturday or no Saturday, I might as well get up.

By the time I had finished getting dressed and had eaten my breakfast, Dad and Bitsey were ready to go tobobeling. In fact, they were ready to go before I had breakfast. . .neither cared if poor, hungry Ernie starved to death. . .all they thought about was getting out to Blunder's Hill. I couldn't figure out which of them was the most excited about the new adventure. They waited for me in the car looking like they'd burst if they had to wait a minute longer. Just as I opened the door to get in, Bitsey jumped out and ran around the corner of the house. She came back immediately, half dragging Claude.

"Claude told me he wants to go tobobeling," she informed Dad.

"Not on your life!" responded Dad firmly.

Bitsey let go of Claude and after arching his bony back at Dad he ran around behind the garage. As we backed out of the driveway I could see Claude peering down at us with a very superior air from his favorite resting place: the cupola on top of the garage roof.

It was a short drive to Blunder's Hill and when we got there it looked like every other kid in Pleasant Valley had also decided it was a perfect day for sledding. Blunder's Hill is a large hill with many different slopes on which you can slide down. Some were short little runs for kids Bitsey's age, but most of them provided nice long rides. In addition, there is the slope known as the "Trail of Death," which is used only by the older and more daring kids.

Dad parked in a long line of cars, then unloaded the two sleds and the toboggan.

"Bitsey wanna ride. . .ride now," cried the little one.

"Not yet, bean bag!" I said. "First we have to pull the two sleds up the hill. Then Bitsey can ride down. It's more fun that way."

"Hurry up," called Dad who was waiting for us at the bottom of the hill with the toboggan. I showed Bitsey how to wrap the rope of her small sled around her hand and off we trudged to where Dad was standing.

"Well. . .which way should we go?" asked Dad in an excited voice.

"How about starting at the top and ending up at the bottom?" I deadpanned.

"Very funny, Ernie," said Dad, but not laughing. "You know very well what I meant. Which slope shall we slide down first?"

"Maybe we'd better begin on one of the middle-size runs," I said, looking at the two of them.

"Bitsey wanna go way up high. . .way up high!" shouted the tobobeling kid as she stared at the kids racing past her at great speed.

"No, I think Ernie's right. Let's begin over there," said Dad, pointing to one of the middle-size slopes. He grabbed hold of Bitsey's free hand and upward and onward the three of us trudged. We were almost to the top of the slope when we heard Bitsey say, "Bye, bye."

"Who are you saying 'bye, bye' to, honey?" asked Dad.

"Bye, bye, tobobel!" announced Bitsey in a sad voice.

"Look Bitsey," I said disgustedly. "We just got here. Stop worrying about going home."

"Bye, bye," she repeated.

Getting through to that kid is something else. I turned

around to try and convince the ding-bat that we were not going, when I noticed a sled just like Bitsey's racing backwards down the hill. . .in fact, since Bitsey's hand was empty, it had to be her sled.

"Oh, no!" I cried.

"What's the matter now?" asked Dad in an irritated tone as he turned around. Bitsey's tobobel ran across a boy's foot, richocheted off a little girl's leg, and then crashed head-on against two boys who were coming down the hill together.

"Bitsey's tobobel went bye, bye," crooned our little angel.

"For heaven's sake, Ernie, don't just stand there with your mouth open. . .go get Bitsey's sled!"

"ME! Why me? It's the ding-bat's fault. She's the one who wanted to see her tobobel go bye bye. Let *her* go get it!"

Dad didn't even answer me, he just gave me the look which says do as you're told or you'll regret it. So I reluctantly started down the hill. I was close to the runaway tobobel, trying to ignore all the hostile stares from those in its path of destruction, when I heard, "Did baby loose her 'ittle, bitty sled?"

"Naturally," I thought. "Why not? I mean, if our sledding adventure begins with a bye-bye tobobel, why shouldn't it also include the colossal thorn in my life. . .John Murphy!"

From past experience I knew that ignoring the idiot simply doesn't work, so I turned around and retorted, "Well, if it isn't John Murphy! I didn't think that Johnny's mommy trusted Johnny to go out of the house by himself, let alone allowing him to go sledding without someone to look after him. My goodness, what would happen if Johnny fell down. He wouldn't know enough to get up without someone to tell him to."

With that said, I grabbed Bitsey's sled, whirled around and beat a hasty retreat back to my family, leaving the megaphone-mouth utterly tongue-tied for once.

"Well," I thought, as I trudged back up the hill. "Maybe that's how to handle the big creep. Maybe that's how I can always have the upper hand with him!" Again, I should have known better. My luck has never been that good.

When I got to the top of the hill, Dad said, "Bitsey had better thank Ernie for getting her sled."

"Good grief!" I thought. "Dad's beginning to sound just like little dopey."

"Thank you, Ernie," chirped the bird brain.

"Just hang onto it after this," I told her, putting the rope around her hand again. "I don't want to have to go after another bye-bye tobobel!"

"Well, now. . ." beamed Dad. "Who's going first?" I could tell he was dying to be first himself.

"Me, me, me," shouted Bitsey. "Bitsey go first!"

"I know," said Dad. "We'll all go together on the toboggan."

"Tobobel. . .tobobel," sang you-know-who. "Tobobel we will go, tobobel we will go. . ."

"Oh, that's just great," I thought to myself. "If John big-mouth Murphy sees me going down with my Dad he'll tease me for the rest of my life."

By now Dad had the toboggan aimed down the hill and Bitsey was climbing on.

"Get in front, honey," instructed Dad. "Then Ernie will get on next and I'll get on at the back." Listen to the expert.

I settled down in back of the twerp and soon felt Dad ease down in back of me. He slid his long legs down the sides so that he was straddling both me and Bitsey.

"Is everybody ready?" sang out Dad. Bitsey chirped a loud and excited yes, and I groaned okay.

"Then," announced Dad breathlessly as he gave a push with his hands. "The Tubb family is off!"

We certainly were off. . .if you can call moving six inches and stopping "off."

"Go. . .go!" screamed Bitsey, clutching at my legs with a death grip.

"I guess I'd better give it another little push," said Dad sheepishly. "Now everyone get ready, for here we go!"

Dad gave a mighty push, and we slid down the hill approximately a foot and a half.

"I suppose maybe I should have waxed the bottom before we left home," he explained with a laugh. "Oh, well, we'll just keep using it until it runs as slick as a whistle."

"I wanna whistle," whined the shrimp.

Dad was too busy pushing with his hands to bother with an answer for her and I was too mortified to do anything but

95

wish I was home in bed. There we were for the whole world to see, and the whole world was right there on the slopes of Blunder's Hill. It's bad enough to ride down the hill with your Dad and his youngest daughter, in full view of all the kids you go to school with, but this...*this* was too much! Dad would push, Bitsey would scream at the top of her voice (which is pretty top!) and the stupid toboggan would move anywhere from two to four feet and stop. That's the way we went down the hill, push...scream...stop...push... scream...stop, while all of the others went whizzing by us laughing their fool heads off. I mean to tell you that we did that push, scream, stop routine all the way down the hill. I've told you before that Dad does not give up easily, and now you know what I mean. We were almost to the bottom when idiot-mouth Murphy flew past us shouting, "You better slow down, or you'll get a nosebleed!" Bitsey got off and cried, "More...more ride...Bitsey wanna do it more!" Dad, who didn't seem the least bit humiliated, laughed and said, "Well, if at first you don't succeed, try, try again." And up the hill he went. Oh, he was trying all right, trying the patience of Ernestine Cecelia Tubb, his disgraced daughter.

For the next forty-five minutes or so Bitsey and I rode down the smaller slopes on our sleds while Dad continued to work on the toboggan. Murphy and his gang didn't bother me anymore because they were all coasting down the "Trail of Death" on the other side of the hill and as far as I was concerned they could stay there, as far away from us as possible.

Then as Bitsey and I were heading up the slope she squealed, "Daddy, look at Daddy." Sure enough, there was our Dad, zipping down a steeper slope on the toboggan with a big grin on his face. "Just like Bitsey," I thought. We watched as he flew past us, reached the bottom of the slope and coasted to a stop. He quickly hopped off and gave us a wave as he started up the slope again, veering off in our direction. He soon reached us and said excitedly, "Let's all try going down together again on the toboggan, only this time, let's begin at the top of the hill."

"You want to go that high?" I asked. "That's next to the 'Trail of Death'...Mom never let Bitsey go that high."

All Dad said was, "Come on, girls, let's go."

Higher meant we would be within eyesight of Murphy and his friends. I knew it was no use trying to change Dad's mind for once he gets it in his head to do something there's just no way to get him to give it up. . .so up we climbed. I was just hoping that the others would be so busy sliding to the bottom they wouldn't even notice us. I didn't think I could bear any more of their remarks today.

When we reached the top, I couldn't believe my good luck. Murphy and his crew had evidently just finished a run down the "Trail of Death," for they were nowhere in sight.

"That sure is a wicked-looking slope," commented Dad, with a certain longing look in his eyes. "Oh, no," I shivered. "He wouldn't seriously think of doing that. . .not with Bitsey along." For once I was glad to have tag-along there.

"It's called the "Trail of Death," I explained to him. "I went down it once last year, but I'll never do it again!" As I have said to you before, I'll never make it as a fortune teller.

The "Trail of Death" slope was the steepest run on Blunder's Hill, but besides just being steep, several other obstacles presented themselves, around which sledders had to maneuver to successfully descend the slope. About midway down there was a two-foot drop-off and beyond that there were several large trees and small bushes. It was scary, to say the least.

"Now," said Dad, positioning the toboggan to go down the other side of the "Trail of Death" slope, "everybody on for the thrill of a lifetime!" He had no idea just how thrilling this ride was going to be.

Now to fully understand what happened next you must realize that the peak of Blunder's Hill is very narrow. To say that it is hardly wide enough to position a sled of any sizable length on top is not an exaggeration. And a toboggan presents an even greater problem, the problem of delicate balancing. Therefore, when Dad put the toboggan down it hung over the top in both directions and looked exactly like a teeter-totter.

"Me first. . .me first!" yelled the creep as she jumped on. The toboggan gave a violent lurch as she did and would have started down the slope if Dad hadn't caught it. "Too bad it didn't," I thought. "Better luck next time."

"Be careful," warned Dad, getting a better grip on it to

steady it. I slowly and carefully lowered my self down behind Bitsey, who already had her eyes closed, ready to do her screaming routine when Dad gave the final push.

Dad was very careful as he got on the toboggan and it seemed for a few brief seconds that our ride might be a pleasant one...that everything would go as planned this time. But I hadn't counted on the Snow Bird opening her eyes at the last minute and seeing a cat way down below that resembled Claude.

"Claudie!" she screamed and in the same instant scrambled off the toboggan before I could grab her.

The following few minutes, which seemed like hours to me, were the most terrifying I had ever experienced in all my life. Within the span of those few minutes I became convinced that my existence in this world was about to be terminated...coming to a swift and sudden end either by being plunged ten feet deep into a snowbank or wrapped around a tree trunk. When Bitsey jumped off the toboggan she unbalanced us...the end she was sitting on went up and the end Dad was sitting on went down. In less than a second, Dad and I were sliding down the slope...but it was the wrong slope! We were sliding down the "Trail of Death" instead of the high slope—and we were going down this slope *BACKWARDS*! Yes, I said backwards...backwards down the most dangerous and difficult-to-navigate slope on Blunder's Hill. Dad yelled something to me but I was too petrified to notice anything but the sound of wind whistling past my ears and the feel of the snowspray as we began our perilous descent. The top of the hill got smaller and smaller. Boy, Dad really had fixed the toboggan so it would move! We flew over the drop-off—THUD!!! The toboggan paused for a second as if to catch its breath, then, with a slight quiver, sped on. The drop had loosened my hold and I lost my sitting position...instead I was lying on my back with my legs up in the air. I could tell that Dad was having a little trouble staying on the toboggan too, for one of his legs was draped across my stomach.

Swooosh!!! The toboggan narrowly missed a huge tree!

Swooosh...Swooosh!!! Two more trees went by in a blur and a flash. Then I felt a tremendous jolt and heard the crash of wood splintering as we careened through one of the bushes along our path. After that we seemed to be going at an even higher speed.

"Dad," I called. "Dad, can't you slow us down? Can't you do something?"

Dad made no reply. Just then one side of the toboggan caught another bush and I was flipped around so that I was facing Dad. . .only there was no Dad. He was no longer riding with me on the wooden death trap. I could now see that I was almost to the bottom. . .but headed straight for another one of those bushes. I crossed my arms over my head and said a quick prayer. The next thing I knew I was lying sideways across the toboggan, clutching what appeared to be several branches from evergreen bushes in my shaking hands. I looked back up the slope and saw some people helping Dad make his way out of a half-demolished evergreen shrub.

We started walking towards each other, but both of us stopped in our tracks as we heard a loud, shrill voice coming from the peak of Blunder's Hill screaming, "I wanna ride the TOBOBEL!"

CHAPTER THIRTEEN

"Dad! Dad!" I hollered as I burst through our front door. I had run all the way home from school to tell him my terrific news.

"Bitsey, where's Dad?" I asked, gasping for a breath of air. Bitsey was sitting on the living room floor making a city out of her blocks, and she finished putting a block in place before she looked at me. She opened her mouth to say something, but by then I heard Dad coming up the basement steps.

"Dad! Dad!" I shouted as I bolted into the kitchen. I startled him so much that he almost dropped the basket of clean clothes he was carrying.

He looked at me with concern in his eyes, "What on earth's the matter, Ernie?"

"Oh, Dad, guess what happened at school today."

"Well, let's see. . .John Murphy kissed you."

"Yuk!" I exclaimed loudly. "Oh, Dad, how could you think of anything like that. Something wonderful happened, not something revolting."

"Yuk, yuk, yuk," echoed the little city planner from the living room.

"In that case, you must have won a million dollars in an essay contest," he responded with a twinkle in his eye.

"Dad. . .be serious."

"I think you'd better just tell me, Ernie," he said as he began chopping up lettuce for dinner.

"Oh, Dad, you'll just never believe it! I can't believe it!"

"Ernie," he interrupted, "just tell me slowly and quietly."

"The most wonderful thing happened. . .the most wonderful thing. . .Mrs. Tucker, our music teacher, chose *ME* to be one of the narrators for our annual spring musical!"

"Ernie, that's great, it really is," enthused Dad, between chops. I could tell he was very pleased and proud, but he'd be a lot more pleased and proud when he saw me in the actual performance.

"And that's not all," I gushed. "Guess who was chosen to be the other narrator!"

"Well, considering your mood, I guess it's not John Murphy."

"Is *he* all you can think about today?" I asked indignantly.

"Okay, Ernie, who's the other narrator?" asked Dad, obviously getting a little impatient.

"It's Louise!" I proclaimed loudly.

"Oh, that's good, honey, she's one of your best friends, isn't she?"

"Louise is my *very best* friend!"

"What's a narbator?" asked the creep, coming into the kitchen.

"Narrator!. . .Narrator!. . .Narrator!" I repeated, hoping that crazy mouth might pronounce a word correctly for once in her life.

Dad stepped in and explained to the pest, "Bitsey, a narrator is the person who is the star of the show. . .the most important person in the whole play."

Although Dad's explanation was not entirely correct, I rather liked it. Besides, when you're trying to explain something to bird-brain you just can't get too technical. Anyway, Dad was sort of correct. After all, Louise and I would both be out in front of either side of the stage, and each of us would have her own microphone. Imagine that! Each of us having her own personal microphone! It was just too good to be true. I could hardly wait for Mom to get home so I could tell her. . .she'd really be excited. Every year since I've gone to the Pleasant Valley Elementary School, she's helped with the programs. Her one special job is to set up the sound system. Mom's an expert in that. She's the only one involved in the whole production who knows anything about it.

My plans were spoiled though, for when the little creep heard Mom coming, she ran to the door and blurted out the news. Well, that's not entirely correct. . .she blurted out her crazy-mouth version of the news.

"Mommy! Mommy!" she squealed. "Guess what happened to Ernie!" She is always telling people to guess what and then never gives them time to guess. She rattled on without taking a break. "Ernie got a star in school today for being a narbator!"

I stood there struck dumb! I ask you, how could the little creep get things so utterly confused? She is simply beyond my imagination!

Mom stood in the doorway with a puzzled look on her

face. . .no wonder. She looked at me and asked, "Oh, did your class put on a style show, Ernie?" She couldn't quite understand.

"What really happened," I said, glaring at the little motormouth, "is that Louise and I were chosen to be the narrators of our annual school spring musical!"

"Oh, Ernie," said Mom, giving me a big hug, "that's absolutely marvelous. Just great. You and Louise!"

It is certainly nice to be part of a family that really understands what it is to have a talented daughter. . .one who, in Dad's own words, would be the *star* of the biggest musical ever to hit the Pleasant Valley Elementary School.

"And Mom, Mrs. Tucker wants you to help again, no one else knows just how to adjust the sound system, you know."

Mom looked pleased. "Oh, she can count on me," she said. "Mrs. Tucker knows that." It was sure nice to know that my very own Mom would make sure our microphones worked just right.

The month of March was spent in rehearsing for the musical, which was entitled, "A Day in the Enchanted Forest." We practiced the songs to be sung during every music period throughout the entire month. The sixth graders, those without speaking parts that is, were supposed to be the mighty trees in the Enchanted Forest. They sang three songs in all: "Little Acorn Nuts," "The Squirrels Are Tickling Me Silly," and "Stretch Out Your Branches to the Sun." Even though Louise and I wouldn't be singing any of them during the performance, we had them memorized from hearing them so often.

By April I guess Mrs.Tucker was beginning to feel panicky so entire afternoons were given over for rehearsals, so that everyone in the whole school could make a concentrated effort to pull the show together.

And it really needed to be pulled together, believe me. The second graders were having the most problems. They were the flowers of the forest and the problem was getting the different kinds of flowers on and off the stage just at the right times. During one rehearsal the daisies came dancing in too early and collided with the tulips who were just beginning to awaken from their winter's rest. I thought Mrs. Tucker would have a heart attack. She kept screaming,

103

"Don't trample the tulips!"

So many trouble spots popped up that the performance had to be set three days past the originally scheduled time. This postponement became the cause for untold anguish for Ernestine Cecelia Tubb, for Mom could not be there. When I told her the new performance date, she cried, "But Ernie. . .it can't be then. . .it just can't be!"

"What's wrong, Mom?" I asked. "It will be better to have it later. Mrs.Tucker says the extra three days will give us the time we need to really polish up all of the episodes."

"No, Ernie, you don't understand," continued Mom. "Those are the days of the national hardware conference. I have to go."

"Oh, Mom, no. . ." I felt like crying. "What'll we do? Who will work the sound system!"

"Now don't worry, honey, I'll figure something out. I'll call Mrs. Tucker right away and explain."

"Mrs. Tucker will have a stroke, Mom, she really will."

Well, Mom and Mrs. Tucker worked it out so that Mom would come to school during one of our practices and show her and Ms. Fizz, our sixth-grade teacher, what to do. Louise and I had to learn how to test the microphones and adjust them for the younger kids who would need them as they sang in the little groups. Everything went beautifully. Louise and I felt like old pros, briefly considering a career on stage. As Mom left she told us that as long as everything was left exactly as she had placed it, no further adjustments would have to be made.

Two days before the musical, Mom took off for her conference. "I really feel bad, Ernie, that I'll miss seeing you, but I know you understand. Anyway, I was there for your rehearsal. That's my big girl, now." Mom knew I was upset. I just couldn't help it. One of the biggest, most exciting times in my life, and my own mother wouldn't be there! At least I could count on Dad. . .and the little big-mouth.

When the actual evening of the performance arrived, I was so nervous and excited that I couldn't eat dinner.

"Come on, Ernie, try to eat a little something," coaxed Dad.

"If I do, I'll throw up!" I told him.

"Well, at least, drink your milk," he said. "That's what all the big TV stars do."

I managed to get some milk down, then asked, "May I please be excused to go get ready?"

Dad gave me a nod. It seemed like an eternity before Dad said to get our coats on, it was time to leave for school. When we arrived, I ran ahead and met Louise back stage.

"Are you nervous?" she asked.

"Are you kidding? I'm so nervous that I think I might get sick the minute the curtain opens."

"Me, too," confided Louise.

"Girls. . .girls," called Mrs. Tucker, who was looking very harried. "Oh, I'm glad you're both here. Now do just as you've done in the rehearsals and everything will be fine. I must go check on the bunnies and the squirrels now. Don't forget, we're all counting on you, Louise and Ernestine, to keep the show running smoothly." Saying that, she turned on her heels and flew off in the direction of the bunnies and the squirrels.

"That's all I needed!" said Louise. "Now I'm more than just nervous. . .I'm scared to death!"

"Louise," I said. "I feel like I have to go to the bathroom."

"Me, too."

"Do we have time?"

"I think so."

With the decision made, we both headed straight for the girls room.

By the time we returned, Mrs. Tucker was lining up the first grade bunnies to go on stage and giving them a last minute peptalk along with additional instructions.

"All of you bunnies. . .listen! I want to be able to hear each and every one of you sing. I want to see which bunny can hop the best. . .I want to see a stage full of hopping bunnies!. . .Oh, Ernestine and Louise, go take your positions on stage now. It's almost time for the curtain to open."

"I think I have to go to the bathroom, again," I whispered to Louise. She gave me an odd sort of look and then we both went to the microphones on either side of the stage.

"CURTAIN!" yelled Mrs. Tucker to the boy in charge of opening them. He pulled with all his might and my microphone got caught in a fold of the curtains and started to topple over. I quickly caught it and put it back in place. . .and so began, "A Day in the Enchanted Forest."

The audience became quiet and hushed. . .then from somewhere in the back of the left corner of the auditorium a loud, shrill voice bellowed, "Hi, Ernie! Bitsey sees Ernie!" The audience burst into laughter and I could have died.

Trying to keep a pleasant expression on my face, I thought, "I'm going to kill her as soon as this is over."

Thank goodness Louise had the first lines, introducing the bunnies. As soon as it became quiet again, she began.

"Welcome to the Enchanted Forest. We're so glad that you could come, because today the inhabitants of our Enchanted Forest are planning a surprise party for the woodchuck family. The first ones to arrive for our party are the bunnies."

This was the cue for the bunnies to begin hopping onto the stage, but nothing happened. So Louise looked at me, then repeated very loudly, "The first ones to arrive for our party are the bunnies." Still no sign of the bunnies. Then from back stage Mrs. Tucker yelled, "HOP!" and the stage was immediately alive with frantically hopping bunnies.

They began singing their funny bunny-hopping song while hopping around the stage. I noticed Brian Murphy, the mouth's younger brother, hopping close to the edge of the stage, looking out into the audience. He obviously saw his parents because he gave a big grin and waved. That was just before he hopped right off the stage and landed on the floor of the auditorium. A loud gasp came from all the people out there that caused the rest of the hopping bunnies to forget what they were supposed to be doing and instead they hopped forward to the edge of the stage to see what had happened to bunnie Brian. Mrs. Tucker ran out on stage, but by then Brian was scrambling to get back up on stage. One of the fathers in the first row lifted him up so that the musical could continue. That done, Mrs. Tucker led the bunnies back off stage to begin all over. When they came back on stage, singing and hopping, bunnie Brian was hopping with a noticeable limp.

The next group on stage was the second grade flowers and then came the third grade birds. Louise was narrator for both of these groups and everything went as practiced. As the

106

third grade birds were flying around the stage trying to decide what they could give the woodchuck family at the surprise party, I decided to turn on my microphone to get it warmed up, for I would introduce the next three grades. I flipped the switch and lightly rubbed my fingernails across the microphone, a trick taught Louise and me by my Mom. Nothing happened, not a sound.

"That's strange," I thought to myself. "Well, maybe it just needs a little more time to warm up."

Giving it about ten more seconds, I tried again. Still no sound, not even a whisper of a sound. I could feel a sick lump begin to form in my stomach!

"Now this is just silly, Ernestine," I told myself. "There has to be some reasonable explanation for this. Maybe the plug has been pulled." I traced the cord along the stage with my eyes and saw that the plug was where it should be. . .snug in its socket. "Oh, no," I groaned, almost out loud. I tried to get Louise's attention, but she was too busy watching the birds fly back to their nests to see me. As soon as they had all disappeared the stage and auditorium became deathly quiet. It was now my turn to introduce the fourth grade weeds. And so in the finest tradition of theatrical personalities, Ernestine Cecelia Tubb stepped up to the dead microphone and began.

"And so we say goodbye to the birds of the Enchanted Forest."

"Your microphone isn't on," Mrs. Tucker told me in a loud, off-stage whisper.

"It's broken," I whispered back.

A hand quickly shot out from behind the curtain, grabbed the microphone and whisked it backstage. I stood there wondering what to do next when the loud, shrill voice again came from the back corner of the auditorium, "Bitsey can't hear Ernie!"

This, of course, brought on another loud fit of laughter from the audience. I momentarilly thought of running off stage and killing myself along with Bitsey, but then that same hand pushed the microphone back on stage. "The microphone is dead. You'll have to speak up in a loud voice," advised Mrs. Tucker. And so once again, Ernestine Cecelia Tubb began her introduction. Only this time I practically

107

yelled so that even the little creep in the back left corner who should have stayed home could hear me.

"And so we say goodbye to the birds of the Enchanted Forest. Goodbye, birds, goodbye. But wait, who do I hear coming next to our lovely Enchanted Forest? Yes, it is. . .it's our wonderful friends the weeds. Now what could our weed friends be bringing to our surpise party for the woodchuck family?"

That was the cue line and fifty-six fourth grade weeds came dancing on stage singing, "It's Wonderful Being a Weed." At the same time Mrs. Tucker shot out on stage with them, grabbed Louise's microphone and danced it over to me. "Oh, saved," I thought.

Since Louise is shorter than I am, I had to raise the microphone before the weeds were finished. This is a very simple process. . .simply unscrewing the holder, adjusting the height, then screwing the holder back tightly. I finished this easily just as the weeds left the stage. I then began the introduction for the firth grade bears and raccoons.

"Thank you weeds, for helping to make it such a nice party for our woodchuck family. . ." Oh, no, it couldn't be happening! As I talked, the microphone began slipping down, becoming shorter and shorter. I couldn't believe it! I had to keep talking into it as I introduced the stupid bears and raccoons who were waiting. I kept stooping lower and lower during the long introduction until by the time I was finished I was squatting on the floor. You can just imagine the laughs this got from the audience.

While the fifth graders were singing in the Enchanted Forest, I tried frantically to fix that blasted microphone. I unscrewed it again, turned it the other way, tightened up the screw again, but it didn't hold. . .just slowly slipped down again. I repeated the entire process, but the same awful thing happened. I looked over to Louise and she gave me a worried but helpless look. Then it was time to introduce the sixth grade. Another long, long introduction. . .another slowly, slowly sliding movement of the microphone. I couldn't hold it up. . .each time I tried, it would slide down again hitting the bottom with a clunk. . .up, down, clunk. . .up, down, clunk. . .up, down, clunk! While the sixth graders were singing, Ms. Fizz climbed up on stage to help. She did everything I had done...and got the same disgusting results...nothing could be done. I still had the concluding remarks to make and I was so embarrassed it was all I could do to remember what I had to say. I almost collapsed with relief when the curtains came together.

Everyone was very sympathetic and tried to comfort me, telling me I had done very well, that it wasn't my fault something had gone wrong with the microphone. I knew, though, if Mom had been there, she would have fixed it. But no, she was where Dad should have been, not here, helping as she always did. She would have known what to do to save me from all of this humiliation and shame. "Well, at least it's over," I thought...another mistake. John Murphy walked by in his bear costume, and while he didn't say or do anything right then, I knew from the look in his eye that he would never let me forget the tragedy of the sliding microphone. I was too embarrassed to look at anybody, even Louise. I ran to meet Dad and the creep. Bitsey ran up to me, put her arms around my legs, and said, "Ernie...you were a funny, funny narbator!"

CHAPTER FOURTEEN

I was awakened from a sound sleep on a Saturday morning in May by strange scraping noises which seemed to come from Mom and Dad's bedroom. I sleepily staggered out of bed, into the hallway, and stood staring into my parents' room. There was Dad, shoving all of the furniture into the middle of the room. He saw me standing there and shouted, "Well, Ernie, it's about time you were up. Today's the day we're going to scrub this old house from top to bottom!"

"Oh, no," I groaned. "By 'we' I suppose you mean me?"

"Now, Ernie, don't be grumpy. Our family works best when we work together and share the chores. You know that."

Share the chores! Boy, it seems like Ernestine Cecelia Tubb always gets the "lion's share" around here—but I knew it was no use to complain, so I got dressed and, after a quick breakfast, went back upstairs to get my instructions. Boy, oh boy, you'd have thought that Dad was organizing a trip around the world for the Tubb family the way he was carrying on. I don't think I've ever seen him quite so excited or enthused about anything, except maybe when he was all caught up in planning our "old-fashioned" holidays.

"Come on downstairs with me, Ernie," ordered Dad. "We have to get some buckets and old rags so we can get started cleaning right away. No sense in wasting time."

"But Dad," I tried explaining, "This cleaning sure sounds like a lot of work to me. What's the matter with the house the way it is?"

"What's the matter with the house the way it is?" he repeated. "Why just look at it—it doesn't sparkle! You only think it's going to be hard work because you've heard your mother complain about it so often. Why, we're going to get this old house so clean it will look like new!"

"I think I'd rather live in a pleasant semi-dirty house and forget all about this kind of house cleaning," I answered, thinking of how much work he was lining up for me to do.

"Oh, Ernie," said Dad. "Just wait until you begin to see how much difference it will make in our house. With a little elbow-grease it'll look like new!"

I wanted to tell him that he was beginning to repeat himself in his excitement but thought better of it. Just then

111

Mom came into the kitchen, followed by Bitsey.

"Bitsey wanna kiss!" demanded the little creep. She can't stand it if someone tries to leave the house without giving her a goodbye kiss.

"Sure, honey," said Mom, as she bent low to receive a Bitsey sloppy smack. You really need a towel when the juicy kisser gets finished planting one on you.

"Say, honey," Mom said to Dad, "Bitsey wants to paint at her easel in her room this morning. Don't forget to make sure she wears her painting smock and has the plastic sheet on the floor under her."

"Have I ever forgotten?" asked Dad, a bit irritated at the thought that he might need reminding.

"Well I just thought that you might forget in all your excitement about cleaning today."

"There's no need to make fun of me," said Dad, giving Mom an upset stare.

"Oh, I'm not making fun of you," soothed Mom. "I'm tickled to death that you're looking forward to it so much. By the way, did you see this morning's paper?"

"No. . .no time, too busy getting organized," said Dad.

"Well, have a look at this," said Mom, opening the paper to one of the center pages. "Have you ever seen a better-designed ad than this one?" asked Mom proudly.

I leaned over so that I could also see it. In bold face type was printed "ONE DAY SPECIALS AT TUBB'S HARD-WARE STORE." Beneath this headline were about two dozen items that were reduced in price.

"Wow," said Dad. "This should bring in the customers today. Where did you get the idea for this?"

"I'd like to say it was my own original idea, but I saw one something like this at the hardware meeting last month," Mom explained with a smile. The hardware meeting last month (she didn't even glance at me when she mentioned it) was the cause of all of my troubles at the annual school musical. I still flinched every time I thought of those microphones.

"I just thought it might help business," said Mom proudly.

In spite of my painful recollection of that night, I had thought at that moment of another of my "Ernie Specials," a way to get out of helping Dad clean.

"Hey, Mom," I wheedled. "With all the business your ad will bring in, you'll probably need some extra help. I can be ready to go in a half a minute."

"Ernie wants to be a rock girl again," butted in the little twerp.

"Thanks, Ernie," replied Mom. "But I think I can handle it okay today. Besides, your father needs you here at home much worse than I need you at the store." I could tell by the pained expression on her face that she remembered all too well that disastrous day of the inventory sale last January.

"Bitsey wanna paint," piped up the ding-bat.

"Okay," said Dad. "Bitsey is going to paint."

"Well, I'm off to the store," said Mom. "See you tonight."

"Good luck," hollered Dad as she walked out the back door.

"Bitsey wanna paint. . .Bitsey wanna paint *now*!" whined the budding artist.

"Okay, Bitsey, okay," said Dad. "Ernie, while I get Bitsey started you can begin to clean out the basement, then I'll get right to work upstairs."

"Oh, goodie, goodie," I thought. "Just how I've always dreamed of spending a Saturday. . .cleaning out the basement!"

Down I trudged. Dad yelled after me, "Why don't you begin with the walk-in closet, Ernie. Carry everything out of it so we can scrub the floor clean."

"Work, work, work," I muttered under my breath. "Yuk!" I said out loud when I pulled up the latch and opened the closet door. Boxes and sacks were piled on the shelves and covered most of the floor—it was just crammed full of things all sizes and shapes.

"This is going to take me all day just to clean out this stupid mess," I told myself. I figured that I might just as well get started for I sure didn't see any way of getting out of it. I hardly knew where to begin, but an old broken floor lamp seemed to be holding back several boxes and sacks on the nearest shelves so I decided to tackle that first. It wasn't very heavy, but it was very awkward to get it out because of the dumb closet door. It wouldn't stay open, but kept swinging shut and hitting me in the back. Working hard, I managed to maneuver the lamp out of the closet and paused to rest when

Dad hollered down from the kitchen.

"Ernie. . .Ernie!"

"Yeh, I hear you," I answered unenthusiastically.

"Ernie, we need some sponges and wall paper cleaner, so I'm going to run down to the store and pick them up. I won't be gone too long. Bitsey's in her room painting so she shouldn't bother you. Bye," he said, going out the back door.

"Bye," I hollered back, thinking, thanks a lot for asking if I'd like to get out of here and go to the store—no, I should stay here drudging away—I was beginning to understand how Cinderella must have felt. I could hear the mad artist up in her room, for the laundry chute to the basement comes from her room straight down beside the closet. She was singing one of her made-up songs. . .this one happened to be about a frog named Frankie.

"Oh well," I said to myself. "The slave had better get back to her work in the dungeon."

For the next few minutes I carried load after load of stuff out of the closet and everytime I carried something out that stupid closet door which opened into the closet hit me in the back. I don't mind telling you that I had had it with that dumb door, so on about the fifth or sixth trip I gave it a kick that made it nearly fall off its hinges. "That'll fix you, you dumb door," I said. "You better behave now!" Well, I had no more than gotten the words out of my mouth before that dumb door swung back with just as much force as it had swung to, actually shaking the remaining items on the shelves. Bitsey must have heard the noise because I noticed that she became quiet and then began singing another of her made-up songs, something like "Bang, bang, bang, boom, boom, boom, bangedy-bangedy-boom!"

Well, what happened next was the beginning of the lowest ebb in the tide of Ernestine Cecelia Tubb's frightful, disaster-laden, messed-up year! Ernie, the workhorse, gathered up another load of stuff to carry out of the closet, but Ernie, the workhorse, only carried the load of stuff to the closet door. I freed one hand to pull open the door again as I had been doing all morning, but would it open? It would not! It was stuck, and I mean really stuck. I put everything down and pulled with both hands. Still stuck! I put one foot against the wall and pulled again with both hands, giving a good hard yank. Yes, I gave it such a good hard yank that I pulled the doorknob right off, and went crashing back against the opposite wall into a stack of blankets! I just lay back, stunned and unbelieving. This couldn't have happened, it just couldn't. When the door slammed back with such force the latch must have fallen in place. There I was. . .a prisoner in my own dungeon!

Then, floating down from two flights above, came the sound of Bitsey's voice singing, "Bang, bang, bang, boom, boom, boom, bangedy-bangedy-boom!"

"Ernestine," I reasoned to myself, "if you can still hear Bitsey then she should be able to hear you." So I edged as close as I could to the edge of the door and hollered, "Bitsey. . .Bitsey!"

I listened anxiously for some response, but heard nothing . . .nothing but a dead silence. I tried again. "Bitsey!"

Still no response, not even a whisper. I began to wonder if I had suddenly gone deaf.

"Alright, Ernestine," I told myself. "You're going to have to scream your fool head off to get some response from the little ding-bat."

"BITSEY!! BITSEY!!. . .CAN YOU HEAR ME?" I screamed at the top of my lungs.

From two flights above me I heard a tiny voice call, "Ernie. . .is that you, Ernie?" "Well, hallelujah," I thought, "I haven't gone deaf after all."

"YES, BITSEY. . .IT'S ERNIE. . .AND I NEED SOME HELP!"

"Ernie," a very shaky vocie asked. "How did you get in the wall?"

"Bro-ther!" I thought. "Well if the twerp is going to ask such a stupid question she deserves a stupid answer."

"A GREAT BIG, MEAN ROBBER HAS TIED ME UP AND STUFFED ME IN THE WALL!"

I chuckled at my cleverness. . .but not for long. Before I could really explain what had happened, the little creep began screaming. And I don't mean just ordinary ear-piercing head-splitting, Bitsey screaming. . .oh, no. This was screaming that started at the bottom of her toes and gained volume as it passed through her quivering body until it escaped from her mouth that must have been stretched into the shape of a giant letter "O." I'm quite certain that her screaming voice carried to the far corners of Pleasant Valley. If that wasn't bad enough, I heard her running out of her room, racing down the stairs and out the front door, still screaming wildly as if the devil himself were after her!

"Bitsey," I yelled, hoping to stop her. "Bitsey...Bitsey...come back...come back...Bitsey, I was only kidding!" But it was no use...by then I could hear her out in front of the house screaming for help...

"HELP...HELP...A BIG ROBBER...HELP...HELP... ERNIE...MEAN OLD ROBBER HAS ERNIE...HELP... HELP!!!"

There I was locked in the basement closet, totally helpless listening to the screaming midget. Her crazy-mouth screaming never stopped...I mean, she never even slowed down...that is, until the sirens began to wail. Yes, that's right, two big, loud sirens on top of two big police cars, drowning out the noise of the ding-bat's voice!

Flocks of curious neighbors and passersby turned out to see why the police cars had come...to see what was going on at the Tubb's house. They didn't have to wait long to find out. I heard the front door crash open and hurried footsteps clomping around on the first floor and going upstairs to the bedrooms. Then I heard the slam of another car door and Dad's voice calling, "Let me through...let me through." He came rushing into the house yelling something about the basement. Immediately all the clomping came down from the second floor to the first, then down the basement steps...it sounded like hundreds of feet all coming my way. I figured all of Pleasant Valley had turned out in response to Bitsey's screaming. I had a great longing to disappear or at least hide momentarily by crawling into one of the large cartons lining the wall, but knew I would have to face the world sooner or later...and if I waited until later I would probably have the FBI to deal with as well as our local police force. Therefore, Ernestine Cecelia Tubb braced herself for what was to come and said weakly, "I'm in here...in the closet."

"Stand back!" ordered one of the policemen.

"Throw out all of your weapons and don't try any funny business. We've got you covered!" growled another one.

"Ernie!" hollered Dad. "Are you alright, Ernie?"

"Please, mister!" said a policeman. "We'll take care of this!"

"Whoever you are in there. . .you'd better come out now or else we'll have to get tough!"

I started to cry. . .it was all too much. . .all too humiliating! "I'm in here alone. . ." I managed to say between sobs, "and I can't come out cause the door knob came off and the latch fell down and I'm locked in!" I didn't know if they could understand anything I was saying because by that time I was crying so hard that I was shaking all over.

The door flew open almost at once and spotlights shone into my face with a dazzling glare. One of the policemen pulled me out of the closet while another rushed past me with his gun in his hand and searched the crowded little area.

"There's no one here. . .no one at all!" said the second policeman.

"What is this, little girl," asked the other. "Is this some kind of a joke? Well, it's not very funny, if it is!"

I ran sobbing into Dad's arms. He patted my shoulder and kept saying, "Everything's all right now. Ernie. . .everything's all right." The rest of this horrendous nightmare remains mercifully clouded in my mind. I vaguely remember taking some pills Dad gave me, going outside for a minute, then going upstairs to my room and lying down on the bed, and then. . .nothing. Nothing that is, until I was shaken awake by Mom.

"Ernie. . .Ernie. . ." she was saying. "Wake up, honey. . .it's time to eat."

With her help I stumbled downstairs to the dining room. Dad was bringing in hot rolls and a delicious-smelling casserole. The screaming mimi was already sitting at her place, right across from mine.

"Ernie. . .Ernie. . ." she squealed. "Ernie's a star! Ernie's a star!"

I ignored her. I didn't even look at her as I sat down at the table. It was no use, she didn't shut up, but kept right on with her big-mouth squealing.

"Ernie's a star! Ernie's a star!"

"Can't you ever make any sense?" I asked. "What are you babbling about now?"

"She means this," said Mom, showing me the front page of

117

The Pleasant Valley Evening Gazette. I looked at it briefly, then looked again.

"Oh, no. . .no!" I moaned. "No. . .no!"

For there, right there in front of my eyes, on the front page of the local newspaper read by everyone in town, was my picture! There was Ernestine Cecelia Tubb, real as life, wearing the most dazed expression imaginable, standing next to one of the policemen who had come thundering down to the basement. . .but that wasn't all. That was enough. . .but that wasn't all. There was a caption above the picture which read: "Ernestine Tubb Locks Self In Closet." And, if that wasn't embarrassing enough, the following lines were beneath the picture: "Early this morning, this local youngster found herself assigned the unpleasant task of cleaning the closet in the basement of her family's home. In a fit of anger, she kicked the door causing it to slam shut and lock from the outside. Ernestine then called to her sister, Bitsey, age three, and informed her that robbers had locked her in. Bitsey, a quick-thinking little girl, immediately ran to get police help. However, when police arrived and searched the house, a tearful Ernestine admitted it was all a hoax and that she was alone in the locked closet. We suggest, Ernestine, that next time you don't want to clean the closet, just tell your parents and it will be a lot less trouble for everyone."

"Oh, Mom. . .Dad. . ." I was ready to cry again. "It didn't happen that way. . .it didn't!"

"It's all right, Ernie," comforted Mom. "We know you wouldn't deliberately cause all that trouble."

"That's right," agreed Dad. "But somehow strange things happen to you. You'll have to learn to live more carefully."

"Learn to live more *carefully*. . .hah!" I thought to myself. If I lived more *normally*, with my parents doing the *normal* thing they were supposed to be doing, these things wouldn't be happening to me. Dad would be at the store where he belonged, not getting me all involved in his house cleaning plans, and Mom would be here doing the cleaning herself. Oh well, thank goodness the year of the switch was almost over. . .it wouldn't be long until the Tubb family life was restored to its old pattern. Thank goodness! I could hardly wait!

CHAPTER FIFTEEN

I'd just come home from a visit at Louise's house and poked my head into the kitchen to say hello to Dad. I found the room spic and span, but deserted.

"That's strange," I thought to myself. "Dad's usually out here starting dinner by now." I looked in the oven, but it was empty.

"Dad!" I called anxiously.

"In the living room, Ernie."

There he was, stretched out on the sofa reading a book.

"Oh, Dad, what's the matter?" I asked. "Are you sick?"

"Nothing's the matter, Ernie," he assured me. "I'm just relaxing while the clothes are drying."

"But what about dinner, Dad?"

"Ah, you and Bitsey and Mom and I are all going out to dinner tonight. The Tubb family is going out to celebrate!"

"Celebrate? What are we going to celebrate? What?" I asked curiously.

"Just be patient, Ernie, and you'll find out," he said with a chuckle.

"But Dad, I can't wait. I want to know now. Right now!" I cried impatiently.

"Okay, Ernie, I'll tell you just one thing about tonight. We're going to eat dinner at the Victorian Terrace. Now, don't ask any more questions."

"But Dad," I complained. "Can't you even give me just one little hint?"

"Absolutely not!" he said good-naturedly. "You and Bitsey will both find out tonight after dinner."

"Oh, Dad. . .that's hours away!"

"Well then," he returned, "you'll just have to wait out those hours."

"I bet I know," I said, looking him in the eye. "It's to celebrate school being over."

"Good grief, Ernie," he said with a snort. "It's nothing like that. This is a celebration for something really big. . .but that's all you're going to get me to say."

Just then the clothes dryer buzzed and Dad got up and went to the basement.

"Humph!" I said to myself. "He may not think getting out

119

of school is something really big, but I certainly do. . .brother! Whenever something happens so that I don't have to see and hear, especially *hear*, that stupid John Murphy five days a week. . .then there is definitely a need to celebrate, whether my Dad thinks so or not! But I was really curious. . .the Tubb family rarely goes out to eat, in fact we hadn't done so once since Dad took over the kitchen. What could it be that we were going to celebrate? And we weren't going to eat at just any place, but we were going to the Victorian Terrace, the nicest supper club in all of Pleasant Valley. I had never been there, but Louise's grandmother took her there on her birthday and she told me how absolutely divine it was. She said there was even a man who strolled around from table to table playing your favorite songs on his violin. I could hardly wait to go. . .and I was sure curious about what the Tubb family was celebrating. Well, regardless of what the rest were celebrating, I was going to enjoy my own private celebration of the ending of the school year.

"Ernie, play with Bitsey and Claudie," pleaded the little creep as she came into the living room, carrying her favorite companion.

"Aha," I thought to myself. "If the mouth knows the mouth tells."

"Bitsey," I asked sweetly. "Did Dad tell you what we were celebrating tonight?"

"No," she answered. Then she added, "Why is Daddy selling something?"

Now that was my fault. You see I used a four syllable word when ol' crazy-mouth can't usually even handle the one syllable words yet.

"Bitsey and Claudie want to play hide and seek," she continued. "Ernie, you play too."

"Okay," I agreed. "But just for a short while, a *very* short while. You and Claude go hide while I count up to fifty."

"Come on, Claudie!" she screamed. Claudie had no choice but to go along as the ding-bat still had him clutched in her arms. She raced up the stairway to her very favorite hiding place. . .to her *only* hiding place. . .her bedroom closet. That's right! Every time Bitsey plays hide and seek she always hides in the same place. Now do you see what I mean about being dumb! Oh, well, that's Bitsey. So I began counting. . .1, 2, 3, 4, 5, 10, 15, 20, 30, 40, 50. . ."Here I come, ready or not!" I hollered in the direction of the stairs.

"I'm coming now," I yelled as I climbed the stairs. I clomped up the steps so she would hear me coming and have a chance to get Claude and herself safely into the closet.

"Gee. . .I wonder where Bitsey and Claude could be," I said as I entered her bedroom.

I heard a muffled giggle and a strangled meow from behind the closed closet door.

"Oh. . .I wonder if Bitsey and Claude could be hiding under the bed?"

"No," came a squeaky voice from the closet.

"Oh, good grief!" I thought. "Just how dumb can you get?"

"Well, then. . .I wonder if they're behind the drapes?"

"No," came the same squeaky voice again, accompanied by another strangled meow.

"Then they must be hidden in the closet," I said as I opened the door.

"SURPRISE!" screamed the hide-and-seek queen at the top of her voice.

Now can you imagine that? The twerp yelled "Surprise" as if no one could have guessed where she had been hiding.

"We surprised Ernie, Claudie," cooed Bitsey. "Let's play again, Ernie."

Just then I heard the car pull into the driveway.

"Mom's home," I said to the little nuisance and we both raced down the stairs and outside to greet her.

"My goodness," said Mom as she walked along the driveway. "It's not every day I'm greeted by a welcoming committee. What's up?"

"Oh, Mom," I said, "you've just got to tell me what the big surprise is that you and Dad have for us. I just can't wait until after dinner. I can't."

"So. . .that's the reason for my welcoming committee!"

"What's Daddy and you gonna sell, Mommy?" asked the little ding-bat.

Mom just stood there staring at her with a puzzled look trying to figure out what crazy-mouth meant this time.

"What do you mean, honey. . .sell?" asked Mom.

"She's mixed up as usual," I said, giving Mom a disgusted

look. "I told her that we were going to celebrate tonight and so now she thinks that we are *selling* something."

"No, no, we're not selling anything," laughed Mom as she walked into the house with the two of us following her. "And as for you, Ernie, it's too bad, but you'll just have to wait for the surprise until after dinnner."

Boy, did time ever drag then, but eventually, after what seemed like days, the four of us were seated in our car driving toward the Victorian Terrace. Mom and Dad were still acting very mysterious about their surprise, never giving a hint as to what it was all about. I resigned myself to waiting until after dinner and decided to share what I knew about the Victorian Terrace.

"Louise told me that there is a man who walks around to the tables while you eat playing the violin, and you can ask for your favorite song," I said in an effort to stimulate some conversation about the restaurant.

"Yes, that's right," said Mom. Then she added, "It's a very nice restaurant and we will all have to watch our table manners."

That last remark of course, was for the little creep's benefit, for everyone knows that my manners are superb.

"The name of the restaurant is the Victorian Terrace," said Dad patiently.

"Billy has a dog named the same as the rest of the runts," was Bitsey's response.

"Oh, bro-ther!" I said in disgust. "How long do we have to put up with her dumbness? I'm sure Billy's dog is named the Victorian Terrace like the 'rest of the runts'!" I was about to add that that was the dumbest of all the dumb, really dumb things I've ever heard her say, but I thought better of it when Mom turned around and gave me a very direct stare.

"Billy said so!" yelled Bitsey. "He said she was a terrace!"

"Quiet down, Bitsey," commanded Mom. "Are you sure that Billy didn't say that she was a terrier?"

"That's what I said. . .that's what Billy told me, she's a terrace."

"Oh, good grief," I said. "She never listens to anything!"

"Never mind, Ernie," said Dad.

I was still muttering to myself as Dad turned the car into a driveway which curved up to a high white-pillared building.

He stopped the car in front of a sidewalk covered with a dark red carpet that led up to huge white double doors with gold doorknobs. As soon as the car stopped, a man dressed in a blue uniform opened the door for Mom, who got out, followed by Bitsey and me. The same uniformed man walked around the car, gave Dad something, then got into the car and drove it around the building.

"Why did Daddy sell the car to that fleeceman?" asked the twerp.

"No, no honey, that man isn't a policeman. . .he's the doorman, and he's parking the car for Daddy." Mom actually thought Bitsey had said something clever and was still laughing when Dad joined us.

"Come on, girls," said Dad. "Let's eat!" He sure was in a good mood. So was Mom.

We went through the big double doors and entered the most beautiful room I had ever seen. I decided that Louise hadn't exaggerated. Everything was decorated in gold, white, and deep red. The carpet was so thick that I felt like I would sink down to my knees in it, and all around the room were white marble statues. I had never seen any place like this. . .it was absolutely lovely. The lights were very dim and I could hear soft music playing in the background. "Oh, how elegant," I thought to myself. I just loved it. At that point I didn't really care why we were there. . .I was just glad to feel a part of the divine atmosphere.

"It's awful dark in here," said Bitsey in that piercing voice which probably carries to the four corners of the world. Several people turned around to look at us. . .I could have just died! Luckily, a lady with some menus in her hand quickly led us to our table. I had to sit across from the little creep, so I gave her my look which says, "don't you dare say anything else." Unfortunately she wasn't looking at me for the piercing voice came again. "Bitsey has to go tinkle!" I just stared at my napkin lying on the table, afraid to look up. . .I knew what was coming.

"Ernie, honey," said Mom in a voice as soft as the lights. "Will you please take your little sister to the restroom?" The way she asked wasn't a request but a command. I had no choice, but tried anyway.

"I don't know where it is," I said, not taking my eyes off the napkin.

"Bitsey has to go tinkle. . .now!" said the ding-bat even louder than before.

"The restroom is close to where we came in," said Mom. "You won't have any trouble finding it."

"But Mom. . ." I tried again.

"Ernie," said Dad in a warning voice, so I gave up and got up, grabbed the little creep's hand and away we went to go tinkle.

I got her into the restroom as fast as I could and headed her into a stall. She closed the door and locked it. There I stood looking into the wall mirror waiting for her highness to finish. Finally, after what seemed like hours, her ladyship said, "I'm finished, Ernie."

"Congratulations," I said. "Now will you please come out so we can go back to our table and get our dinner?"

"I don't know how to get out!"

"What do you mean you don't know how? Just push the little knob on the door."

I heard a few rattles at the door, but nothing happened.

" I can't do it," she called, and I could tell that she was about ready to cry.

"Oh, good grief, Bitsey, don't cry. Ernie will get you out of there."

Yes, good old Ernie to the rescue once again. Are you ready for what Ernestine Cecelia Tubb was forced to do next to free her little sister who had trapped herself in the restroom stall? I mean. . .forced to do in her very nicest dress, the nicest dress she had ever owned? Well, Ernestine Cecelia Tubb got down on her stomach and crawled under the door of the stall! That's right. . .crawled under the door of the stall, praying that no one would come into the restroom at that very moment. Well. . .luck was with me for once, which is unusual to say the least. I managed to crawl under without any problems and help Bitsey out without anyone coming in to witness my acrobatics.

Once out, I looked at the ding-bat and told her, "Now, listen to me very carefully, Bitsey. We are going to leave this restroom and you are not going to say one word. . .not *one* until we get back to our table."

"But, Ernie you got. . ." she started to say.

"No, Bitsey, starting right now. . .not one word!"

"Okay," she said.

"Now I really mean it!" I continued in my sternest, no-nonsense-from-you-manner. "I don't want to hear even a peep out of you."

"Okay," she repeated, staring at me with wide-open eyes.

"Because if I do, Bitsey. . .something dreadful will happen to you. . .something just dreadful!"

"Okay," she whispered as she continued to stare at me. In the same low whisper she asked, "What will happen?"

"Oh. . .something.. .something just awful!" I said, evading her question.

"Will my nose get long like Bambi's?"

"That was Pinocchio's nose, you ding-bat, and yes. . .that's exactly what *will* happen to you."

With that understanding we left the restroom and slowly made our way back to our table. But something was wrong, for as we walked by the other tables I noticed that some people would look at us, then looked at each other and smiled. . .some even laughed. . .others would point and giggle, while the rest just turned and looked. Pretty soon it seemed as if everyone in the Victorian Terrace had their eyes on us as we walked back to our table.

"Now what has the little creep done?" I wondered to myself. I could feel my face turning red as I hurried her highness along. When we reached our table I sat down as quickly as possible, staring down at my ruby red napkin which was the exact same color as my face. I said very quietly and calmly, "Don't ever ask me to take that little creep to tinkle again. You wouldn't believe what she did."

"Well, whatever it was, Ernie, it couldn't possibly top what you did," said Mom. I looked at her, then at Dad. . .they were both trying not to laugh, but the tears were runnin down Dad's cheeks and his whole body was shaking.

I didn't understand. . .all I had done was to rescue the dumb little fuzzy-brain. "What do you mean?" I asked.

"Look down at the floor," said Mom.

I stared in disbelief. I was speechless, unable to say a single word. I just stared. There, stuck to the bottom of my shoe was a streamer made of toilet paper. Now I don't mean just a small piece of toilet paper. Oh, no! What I saw was a streamer that would have looked impressive in a Fourth of July parade. It started at my right foot and trailed back, twining around all the tables we had passed. I hoped I'd sink completely down into the thick carpet out of sight of everyone there. "Bitsey," I said, between my teeth. "Why didn't you tell me that I was dragging toilet paper along on my foot?"

Her lower lip was beginning to quiver and she said in her piercing voice, "I didn't want my nose to get long like Snow White's." I just groaned. . . .she was impossible!

"Oh, honey," said Dad to Mom "Let's tell them now why we're celebrating by eating here tonight."

"Maybe we'd better," agreed Mom. "I think Ernie could do with a little cheering up."

"Well, Ernie and Bitsey," began Dad. "Your mother and I have both been so happy this past year and everything has worked out so well at the store and at home that we've decided to make our one-year experimental arrangement permanent. That is, your mother will continue to manage the hardware store and I'll continue to take care of the house."

"Oh, Dad," I said, laughing weakly to humor him. "That's not funny. . .that's nothing to joke about, that won't cheer me up. I can't think of anything worse!" Then it dawned on me—I thought of the reason for the celebration.

"Oh, it's over. . .the year's over isn't it? The year of your job switch is over. That's great, really great! Oh, thank goodness, now we can get back to normal again!"

I was really pleased with myself for figuring it all out. But then I noticed that Mom and Dad were looking at me with dismay.

"Oh, dear. . .oh, Ernie," said Mom sadly. She looked at Dad and said,"Honey, explain it to her."

"No, Ernie, we are not going back to what you call 'normal'! What's normal for your mother and me is to keep living the way we did this past year. We're not joking, we're very serious. . .it's the best way for all of us. You'll see."

"Come on, Ernie," said Mom. "It hasn't been all that bad for you—just think about it."

I've heard that when a person is drowning, his whole life flashes before his eyes. . .well, that's exactly what happened to me at that moment. All of the dreadful, awful, embarrassing incidents which I had gone through during this past year flashed before *my* eyes, one after the other. I shivered in horror! Dad reached over and patted me on the shoulder, and said, "Ernie, you must realize that this past year has been one of learning and adjustment for all of us. Maybe some mistakes were made which bothered you, but next year will go a lot smoother...we'll be a lot better organized. Come on, now, cheer up, this is a celebration. A happy time!"

A happy time...a celebration...just when I had felt saved from another year like this one...it was so close...and now, now all I had to look forward to was a continuing series of disasters. There was only one faint glimmer of hope. Next year would have to be better. It would have to be better for one very simple reason...it absolutely, definitely couldn't be any worse!

That's what I said...those were my very own words ...that's what I thought...it couldn't be any worse, and I kept thinking that comforting thought until the very next week when...but that's another story I'll have to tell you later. . . .